ای دوست

ABOUT THE AUTHOR

Born in Tehran, Maryam Master fled persecution after the Iranian Revolution and escaped the country with her family, arriving in Australia as a refugee at the age of nine. She is a screenwriter, playwright and author who loves creating stories for young people.

Maryam has adapted three of David Walliams' books for the stage – *Mr Stink* (which was nominated for a Sydney Theatre Award), *Billionaire Boy* and *The Midnight Gang* – as well as Oliver Jeffers' *The Incredible Book Eating Boy*, all of which premiered at the Sydney Opera House and toured across Australia.

She began her career in TV, writing for shows like *Home and Away*, *Blinky Bill* and the Jim Henson Company's *Bambaloo*. In 2011 she was selected by Sesame Workshop as the writer for Elmo's tour of Australia.

Maryam is the author of *Exit Through the Gift Shop* – shortlisted for the CBCA Book of the Year for Younger Readers and the ABIA Book of the Year for Younger Children 2022. *No Words* is her second novel.

Also by Maryam Master

Exit Through the Gift Shop

NO WORDS

MARYAM MASTER

PAN
Pan Macmillan Australia

Pan Macmillan acknowledges the Traditional Custodians of country throughout Australia and their connections to lands, waters and communities. We pay our respect to Elders past and present and extend that respect to all Aboriginal and Torres Strait Islander peoples today. We honour more than sixty thousand years of storytelling, art and culture.

First published 2022 in Pan by Pan Macmillan Australia Pty Ltd
1 Market Street, Sydney, New South Wales, Australia, 2000

Reprinted 2023 (twice)

A catalogue record for this work is available from the National Library of Australia

Typeset in FreightText Pro by Astred Hicks, Design Cherry
Cover, text design and illustrations by Astred Hicks, Design Cherry
Author photograph: Kate Williams Photography
Illustration on page 33 from shutterstock
Printed by IVE

The paper in this book is FSC® certified. FSC® promotes environmentally responsible, socially beneficial and economically viable management of the world's forests.

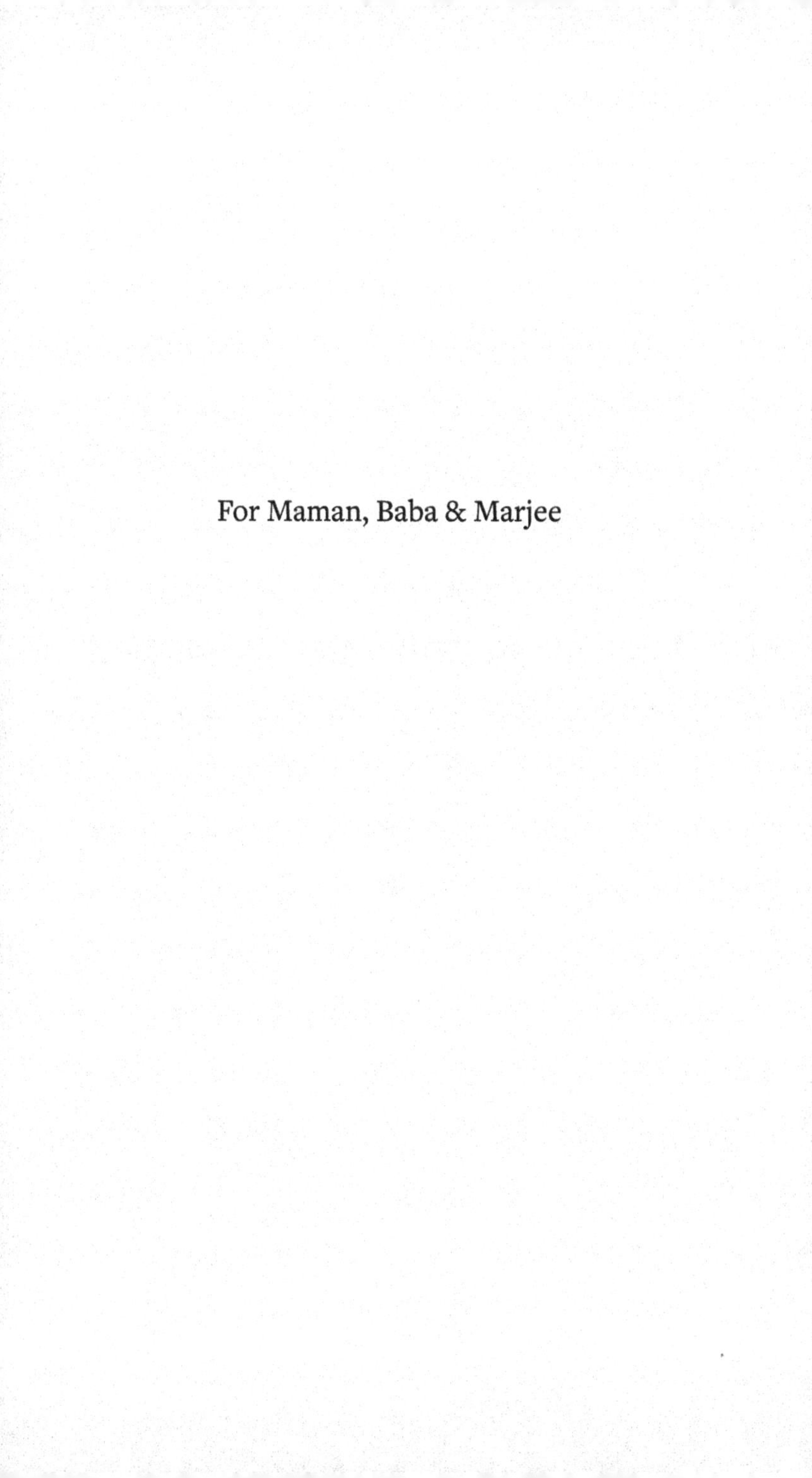

For Maman, Baba & Marjee

HERO

The sun is barely up and I'm sitting in a booth at the 24-hour Macca's up the road. Skye is sitting next to me. She literally spit-sprays some of her caramel milkshake all over the table because she's laughing so hard at Dad. She's too young to be embarrassed by what's going on. Me, on the other hand, I'm pulling my school hoodie over my head as far as it'll go.

Dad is standing on his seat.

Singing.

Opera.

Out loud.

Figaro, figaro, figarohhhhh!

Dad takes a bow. Skye claps. 'Again! Again!'

'No! Please, not again,' I plead as I look around at the bleary-eyed early-risers staring at us. Some look confused by this scene of a middle-aged man singing opera at the top of his lungs to his daughters. Others look annoyed. They've probably come off a night shift and didn't ask for opera with their fries. But most people are amused, either laughing or smiling. Which would be nice, if I knew for sure that they weren't laughing AT him. But I don't know that . . . which is why I ask him to sit down.

'Please, Dad, your hotcakes are getting cold and I know how much you hate not-hot hotcakes.'

Dad's face lights up. You can see the very moment an idea lands in my dad's head. His eyes widen, his mouth curls into a half-smile and the skin on his cheeks lifts up as if it's being pulled by invisible string.

'I've got an idea!'

'Daaaaad! Sit downnn.'

'Who wants hotcakes?'

I tell him that we already have hotcakes but he's not talking to me. He's talking to everyone else. EVERYONE else! He hops off the chair and approaches all the randoms who are trying to enjoy their breakfast in peace.

'Would you like some hotcakes? I'm buying!' says Dad.

'Oh, yes, please,' replies a woman wearing a nurse's uniform.

'Excellent!' Dad then shouts to the 16-year-old cashier. 'One serve of very hot hotcakes for the lady!'

The poor pimply kid looks so confused. Is he supposed to put the order through? Is he being punk'd? Is this *Prank Patrol*?

I wanna tell him that it's not. Just my dad having one of *those* days. But I don't really have time to explain anything to Awkward Macca's Boy. Dad's already moving on . . .

'Who else would like some hotcakes? Don't be shy. This is your moment, people. It's my shout. Hotcakes are on me!'

An old homeless-looking man tentatively puts up his hand. 'I'll have some, if it's not too much trouble.'

'Me too,' says a truckie with a fat moustache in the adjacent booth. 'Please and thank you.'

Skye can't stop laughing. She's having the time of her life. So is Dad. He shouts at Awks Macca's Boy again.

'Two more serves! For my friends over here.'

But that's not enough. Dad wants to buy *everyone* hotcakes. Whenever he's like this, everything is exaggerated. Bigger. Better. Hyper-real. Un-real. Like a movie. I usually love his **UP** moods. But today, I'm tired. And we're in public.

Dad is right up at the counter now. 'I'd like to buy everyone here, including yourself, young man, some very hot hotcakes.'

Awks Macca's Boy looks around the restaurant. Panic sets in as he tries to count the number of people. 'So, that's . . . um, how many, sir?'

'Sixteen. Sixteen serves. Oh, actually, make that 17 because mine are probably cold by now. And I like my hotcakes HOT!'

Awks types in the order. 'That'll be . . . $81.60.'

Dad plonks down his card. And there's a spontaneous round of applause from the people now awaiting their hotcakes.

Dad takes another bow.

He's loving life today. I can't help but smile. I'll take this early-morning-Macca's-madness over sinking-into-the-couch-sadness any day of the week.

Skye leaps up and hugs Dad. He squishes her back.

I gesture for him to return to our table. He listens this time. He slides into his booth seat and smiles.

'It's good to see you happy, Dad.'

He reaches across, lifts my hand and kisses it.

'I love you, my Hero.'

H
e
r
o

That's my name, by the way. I'm not his actual hero. Dad is a massive Shakespeare nerd so he insisted on calling me Hero after one of the characters in *Much Ado About Nothing*.

I squeeze his hand back. Today's a good day.

SNIFF, SNIFF

It was still too early for school, so Dad brought us home after Macca's. Mum gave me a quizzical look.

'How was it?'

I nodded to reassure her that it was okay. Compared to some of his other **UP** days, today was mild. She smiled. Phew. I could tell she was relieved. We do all this communicating without any words. Mum and I have a kind of face code. We can have entire conversations just by reading each other's faces.

Dad wrapped his arm around Mum's waist and did a little waltz around the lounge room. Twirling her, dipping her backwards and catching her just in time. Mum laughed. She was happy to see him happy too.

'All right, Fred Astaire, it's time for me to get ready for work.'

Skye giggled. 'Who's Fred Upstairs?'

'Take the day off and dance with me,' suggested Dad.

'Ha! Those armpits aren't going to sniff themselves, you know.'

Oh, that must sound confusing. I should explain. My mum is an Odour Judge. Yes, you read that correctly. She sniffs armpits for a living. You think I'm kidding? Go ask your friend Google. You can't make this stuff up.

You see, when companies produce new products like deodorants, perfumes and mouth fresheners, they need people to test them. Volunteers try them and Odour Judges are hired to smell their . . .

Breath.

Feet.

Armpits.

They have to gauge whether the products are doing their job in eliminating stench. While most people wear a suit and sit behind a desk in their day jobs, my mum wears a lab coat and polishes her nose senses as part of her get-ready-for-work routine.

Sniffing coffee beans helps you neutralise your sense of smell. So, she does a lot of that. She always skips breakfast because apparently eating before sniffing dulls your senses. And if she has even the mildest cold, she can't work because she needs her full smell powers. Of course, smell is my mum's superpower.

She has to have her sense of smell tested monthly. Just to make sure her supersonic, ultra-bionic whiffa-sniff powers are up to scratch. (Scratch-and-sniff pun fully intended.) Her job may be a **stinky** one. Literally. But she takes pride in it. 'It's honest work,' she says.

So, yes, you could say that my family is . . . eccentric. Skye too. She's only five but she's got her quirks. She likes to eat crayons. And lick walls. She talks to her imaginary friend Thelma like it's no big deal, and every now and then she pretends to be dead, just to see if anyone will notice or care.

I'm the boring one of the family. No strange jobs, habits or moods. Everyone's rock. Hero, the sensible one. The carer. The 'A' student.

Yawwwwwwwnnnn!

If I died today, my tombstone would say:

Here lies Hero Jean Rodriguez. The most exciting thing she ever did was catch a fly in a jar, fill it with water and freeze it to make a fly ice-block. But then she felt so bad that she defrosted it and tried to revive the fly using micro-CPR.

Sad but true.

I wish I could do something exciting. I wish I could live up to my name. Being called Hero is truly a curse. The pressure is intense. I wonder if Usain Bolt ever felt the pressure of *his* name. Did the fastest man on earth ever have slow days? When his feet felt cemented to the ground? Like he was traipsing through sludge? Did he ever come last in a school race? Or was he always a speed demon, a lightning BOLT?

BE CAREFUL WHAT YOU WISH FOR!

By the time I got to school, I was already exhausted. Dad's **UP** days have a way of making me extra tired. So, I was hoping for a quiet, uneventful day. A day where I could just blend into the wallpaper. I know I JUST wished for the opposite. And I did it out loud. In writing, actually. That was silly. I really should know that when you put things out into the universe, the universe responds.

'You wanna be a hero, Hero? Here's your chance!'

RIGHT THIS WAY -->

I was barely through the front gate at school when I saw Aria.

He was copping it again.

Doofus had him in a headlock and was shouting in his face.

High school honestly sucks.

‘What’s that, Mute Boy?! Choo say sumfink?’

Doofus leant right in. ‘Can’t hear ya. Speak up, Mutey! I know you stole my diary, ya little squirt. You tryin’ to get back at me for the wedgies, ay? Genius plan, but it ain’t gonna work. I’m on to you. Give it back right now or you’re gettin’ another one. An atomic wedgie this time. You know what that is? Oh, those are rare. I save ’em up for special occasions. Jockstrap stretched all the way from ya butt crack to ya nose. Classic.’

Aria stared at the ground intently. Looked like he was counting the ants on the concrete.

Doofus laughed like a hyena then cupped his ear, pretending he couldn't hear.

'Beg. Your. Pardoneh? Still can't hear ya, amigo. Where's my damn diary, you little stinker?'

Aria said nothing. He never says anything. Doofus finally released Aria from the headlock.

'In case you've forgotten what it looks like, it's a yellow book about this big . . . with my NAME on it. Rufus. That's R. U. F. A . . . I mean, U . . . I mean, whatever, it's Rufus! RUFUS!!'

Doofus Rufus

Rufus has roughly the same IQ as a block of cheese. Or a doorknob.

Not the sharpest tool in the box, as my mum would say. And he's mean. As you can see. Exhibit A . . .

A textbook bully. A loudmouth, all-up-in-your-face, brainless thug. Doofus Rufus, as I like to call him, is a combination of Draco Malfoy and Biff Tannen from *Back to the Future*. Hair like cauliflower. Cheeks like beetroot.

He's repeating Year 9.

For the 11th time.

Nobody knows his real age. Rumour has it that he's actually 71. He has no real friends at school, just a couple of other dropkicks who follow him around and snort-laugh at his stupid jokes. They're possibly thicker than him. Which is really saying something. Doofus's main hanger-on-er-er is Alfie Toogood. Yes, that's his real name. Although, he's everything *but* good. Too tall. Too dim. Too much of an all-round general loser. Follows his bruiser buddy around like a bad smell, never really saying or *doing* anything. Big waste of space, really.

So, it turned out, Doofus Rufus had lost his diary. Let's just pause here a moment. A diary? Doofus has a *diary*? Like Adrian Mole or the Wimpy Kid, or someone from the 19th century? Just imagine this buffoon going home, sitting at his mahogany desk with a cup of tea and a feather quill, writing his deepest, darkest, dopiest thoughts in a diary. It's jarring, isn't it? But hey, no judgement here. Whatever rocks his socks.

Anyway, he had accused Aria of stealing the precious Doofy chronicles, as part of some sort of wicked revenge plan for all the bullying, which of course can't be true. Aria is just not that kind of boy. He wouldn't hurt a fly. Unlike me (I never did manage to revive that frozen fly).

So here was my chance. My chance to live up to my name. To step in and save Aria. To be a hero.

But I didn't.

Instead, I froze. I became static. Motionless.

My heart started pounding and thoughts raced through my head.

DANGER!
DANGER!
DO NOT,
I REPEAT,
DO NOT
APPROACH
THE BEAST.

I tried to ignore the warning voice inside my mind and took a step towards Aria, but gravity reached up like an invisible octopus and slowly wrapped its tentacles around my ankles. The thoughts kept coming . . .

Who do you think you are? She-Hulk? Get a grip! You're a wuss. A Year 7 newbie. There's nothing you can do. Keep your head down and stay out of it.

It's a jungle out there.

And so, I stood by and watched Doofus push and shove Aria.

I did nothing.

Nobody did anything.

Apparently that's called the . . .

BYSTANDER EFFECT

When you see something bad happen and you do nothing. You literally stand by and watch. By-stander.

Not by-helper.

Or by-call OOO -er.

Or by-whoop Doofus in the noggin and save the day-er.

By-STANDer.

I'm ashamed to say that's just what I did. I stood by and I watched. Hoping someone else would do something – and be the hero.

Butterfly Effect

Of all the 'effects' out there, the 'Bystander effect' is not one to aspire to. Nor is the 'Domino effect'. Everyone gets toppled in that one.

The 'Butterfly effect' is the best of the bunch.

My kindergarten teacher, Ms Gentle, first told me about it.

It's kind of a mind-blowing idea that everything is interconnected somehow. That a butterfly flapping its wings in one part of the world can cause a typhoon in another. Clearly, it can't literally do that. But the point is that every small thing we do – or don't do – causes something else to happen – or not happen. Our destiny is made up of tiny acts, not big, earth-shattering ones. So, everything matters. We are not puny, insignificant nobodies.

We are mighty!

Well, our actions are, anyway.

I actually think this crazy theory is true, which is why I felt a huge surge of guilt come over me as I stood by and watched Aria get pushed around.

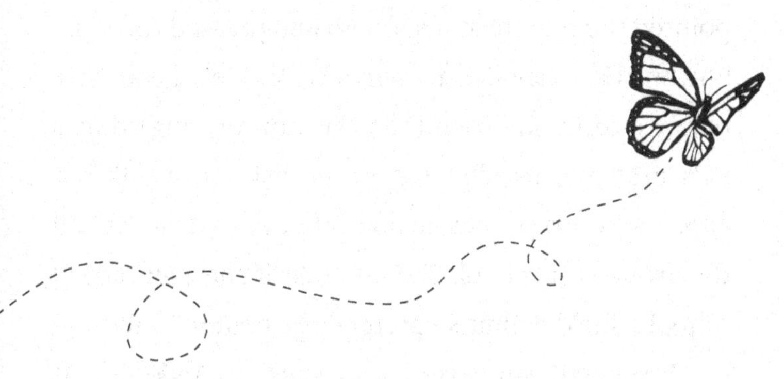

'Mute Boy'

Aria is a mystery.

He has kind eyes. And a sometimes-mischievous smile.

But no words. None. It's literally like someone pointed the remote at his mouth and pressed the mute button. He's new-ish to our school. He's been here nearly a term. My friend Jaz (Jasmin for long) thinks he's pranking us all. That he probably *can* talk but chooses not to so that he doesn't have to deal with all the drongos at school. She says that if she ever moved schools, she'd definitely pretend she couldn't talk.

'Imagine if you never had to speak to ANYONE! It would be 100 per cent awesome!'

Except that I don't imagine things are awesome for Aria. There is a kind of sadness about him. And it must be frustrating not to have words. The teachers, for the most part, are very understanding. Maybe they know something about Aria that we don't, but they don't seem to question his silence. They ask him yes or no type questions. So, he either nods or shakes his head. And they don't treat him like he's terribly different. He does all the same work and gets some of the best grades. Clearly, he's not stupid. He just doesn't speak. Which is the opposite of some people in my school, who just yap, yap, yap all day long without ever pausing to breathe. Jaz thinks most people (including herself!) have a chronic case of **verbal diarrhoea.**

We both agree that Aria's silence is like an oasis. A little island of quiet in a chaotic world of noise. So, the first time we saw him sitting alone on the oval, we decided to go and keep him company. He was eating some kind of rice dish with some gooey brown crud on top that honestly looked like poo. I don't mean to be rude, but it did. Jaz walked right up to him. She's the more confident of us two.

'Wow. What do you call that? Smells delicious. I mean, it looks like crap but I bet it tastes good.'

That was her opening line. Hello, welcome to our school, your food looks like doo-doo.

Aria seemed to take no offence. It's hard to be offended by Jaz. She's so friendly and curious.

And even though her manner is sometimes brash, people don't take it to heart. Aria reached into his bag, pulled out a plastic spoon and casually offered it to her.

'Oooh, yes, please!' said Jaz as she snatched the spoon and hoed into Aria's lunch. I don't know how she does it. She has a way of becoming everyone's instant best friend. Aria watched with some trepidation as Jaz chowed down on the spoonful. At first, she gave nothing away. It was hard to tell if she was going to burst into applause and wipe away a tear at the sheer deliciousness of the brown goo or if she was going to vomit.

Waiting for her response was kind of torturous. Which way will it go? She chewed, chewed, gulped, swallowed and finally, with a sparkle in her eyes, exclaimed . . .

'YUMMMMM!'

Then immediately reached over for another spoonful. Aria smiled big. Really big. I saw his oversized perfect teeth for the first time ever.

'What *is* this stuff? Mmmm . . .' She took over, as she tends to do. Aria sat back and watched with glee as she scoffed down his lunch.

'I know you're not much of a talker, but you gotta tell me what this is, man. Here . . .' She handed him an old receipt and a pen from her pocket. 'Write it.' He jotted something down and handed it back. She read it out loud.

He nodded.

'Dude, I have no idea what that is but I'm gonna google the recipe as soon as I get home. Did you make it?'

Aria shook his head.

'Your mum?'

He shook his head again.

'Dad?'

Aria nodded, looking proud.

'Lucky you have a good chef in the house. My mum is literally the world's worst cook.'

That is actually true. Jaz and her mum live alone. Her dad left when she was teeny so it's just the two of them and Jaz does most of the cooking because, well, frankly, her mum's culinary skills stink. No disrespect. Just facts.

Back to Aria – ever since that lunch-sharing day on the oval, the three of us have become a bit of a gang. Not your average kind of gang, of course. No matching tattoos. No secret handshakes or a treehouse where we have meetings and somebody takes minutes. No plots to take over the world or solve international crimes. But a gang nonetheless. A dorky gang of three misfits.

Hero the anti-heroine.
Jaz the extrovert.
Aria the no-talker.

A weird mix by anyone's measure, but it works. We hang out almost every lunch and recess. Unlike other friend groups, we don't have a usual 'hang' spot. We're mostly on the move so that we can avoid Doofus. He's had it in for Aria since day one and even though Jaz and I are too chicken to actually stand up to him, we try to protect Aria in different ways. By hiding in bushes or in the library or behind the canteen, near the dumpsters. We've contemplated telling the teachers about the bullying but we're currently too chicken for that too. What if that triggers Doofus even more? He's told us on more than one occasion that 'snitches get stitches', which is prison-inmate speak for 'if you dob, I'll bash ya'.

And seeing as Rufus is about twice our size and perhaps ten times our age, we don't dare tell any teachers about how he terrorises Aria. Instead, we play cat and mouse with the school's geriatric bully. If he can't catch Aria, he can't hurt Aria.

Of course, sometimes, like this morning, we fail to shield our friend.

And those days suck.

Scar Finger

Aria has a scar on his middle finger. Yes, the rude one. Three deep dents around the same size. Like stitches. Or staples. Or bite marks. Jaz asked him about it once but, of course, he didn't respond. Not even in writing, which he usually does with us.

You're probably thinking, what's the big deal? Lots of people have scars. All over their bodies. Not every scar has a story and not every story has to be shared. But for some reason, this particular scar on Aria's finger haunts me. Maybe it's because whenever we mention it, his face changes. As if a dark cloud suddenly comes over him. He shuts down and simply shakes his head. Clearly stating, in his wordless way, 'I don't want to talk about it'. I know that's not a terribly unusual response for a boy who doesn't talk, full stop. But still, something about it makes me wonder what he's hiding. What piece of the mysterious Aria puzzle lurks in those three dents?

I want to ask him so many things. What happened to your finger? What happened to your voice? Who are you?

But I know you can't just ask these things. As curious as I am, I know better than anyone that probing questions suck. I hate it when people ask . . .

Hey, Hero, what's wrong with your dad?

Where is he on a scale of 'slightly cray' to 'Tom Cruise'?

Does he need a check-up from the neck-up?

Why's he so down?

Why's he so hyped?

Is he *always* like this?

Sometimes I turn into Mute Girl when I'm being bombarded by too many questions. 'Shut up!' is what

I wanna say to people. None of your beeswax! He's perfectly normal. Just not *your* definition of it.

It's hard to stay under the radar when you're hit by an avalanche of questions. Makes you want to crawl into a hole and hide. So, I'm careful not to hassle Aria. I won't be that annoying nosy person in his life. I will not.

But that doesn't mean I'm not secretly dying to know. Jaz and I will get to the bottom of it one day. We are determined to uncover the Aria story, one way or another.

Aria

I am not mute.

I can speak.

Three languages, actually.

But I don't talk at school.

I can't.

I like Hero and Jaz. They're the nicest kids I've met since I arrived in Australia.

Jaz is funny. She talks a lot.

Hero saw Rufus push me around this morning. She looked scared. I wanted to tell her not to worry. I've been through much harder things. This is nothing.

Miserable Ms Rubble

I had English for the first period. I was late for class 'cause I hung back to make sure Aria was okay after the rumble. He was. Or at least he pretended to be. He dusted himself off and headed to Geography. I bolted towards English, super worried about being late. Ms Rubble, my English teacher, is very strict. She doesn't like latecomers. Or early leavers, for that matter. It doesn't matter if you have a dentist appointment or a funeral to go to. Class time is sacred. If she has to allow anyone to miss a single minute of class, her bushy monobrow curls into a big frown which looks like a big black eagle flying above her eyes.

You do not want to mess with her. When Ms Rubble becomes miserable, all hell breaks loose. And it's not hard for her to lose her cool. Any small infraction can send her into a total spin. There's no room in her class for interrupters, chatterboxes, left-my-homework-athomers or any other kind of slackers. She usually starts the lesson by shouting at us like a military officer . . .

MS RUBBLE:
One, two, three,
eyes on me!

We've learnt the appropriate response. Like well-trained soldiers, we chant back to her . . .

TERRIFIED STUDENTS:
One, two, eyes on you!

MS RUBBLE:
Sit up straight. Homework out. Foe-KAS!

That's how she says 'focus'. Stretches the word out for ages, then brings it home like a gunshot.

So, you can imagine my nerves as I arrived three minutes late for class. My heart was pounding. I wondered if people could actually *see* it pounding . . . *boom, boom, boom.*

But I shouldn't have worried because there was already chaos in the classroom and she didn't even notice me sidling in slightly late.

Somehow, she'd lost control of the class. Kids were whispering to each other and trying not to laugh. Something had happened and not even Ms Rubble's wrath was subduing them.

MS RUBBLE:
KOOO-WHYYYYY-
ETTTTT!!

Her piercing voice and angry scowl hushed them momentarily. But then someone's giggle escaped. And because giggles are contagious, someone else caught it and they giggled too. Before you knew it, there was total, complete giggle-mania again.

Ms Rubble threw up her hands in despair. I slid into the seat next to Jaz.

'What on earth is going on?' I asked her.

Jaz told me that Eloise Pratt had told . . .

Ziyan Ali . . .

who told Phoebe Koch . . .

who told *her* that Rufus Sherman, AKA Doofus Rufus, still wets the bed!

WAIT . . . WHAT?

How could this be true? The guy is way past bedwetting age. He's, like, 102! He can't possibly wet the bed, can he?

Maybe he can.

Maybe he's got a condition.

If this were really true, and not fake news, how could it be public knowledge? So many questions swirled around in my brain. I actually felt sorry for Doofus. Sure, he's a big, bad mean machine, but no one deserves this kind of humiliation. Not even him.

As I tried to absorb this revelation, George Leibowitz, who was sitting on my other side, handed me a crumpled note. It read:

George was cacking himself, so impressed by his own gag. Laughing so hard that snot came flying out of his nose. Thankfully I dodged it.

Ms Rubble's voice went up about 400 decibels.

'The next person to laugh, giggle, talk, whisper or BREATHE is on DETENTION!'

Jaz, who hasn't quite perfected the art of shutting up when one really should, shot up her hand.

Jaz: But, Miss, you can't give us detention for breathing.

Ms Rubble: That's it! Lunchtime detention for you, Jasmin!

Jaz: You can't do that!

Ms Rubble: Shall we make it two detentions?

Jaz: What?!

Ms Rubble: Three it is!

Jaz: That's crazy!

Ms Rubble: Oh, you want me to round it up? Sure! One hundred detentions!

Jaz: A HUNDRED detentions?!

Ms Rubble was mad. Real mad. She later took back the 100 detentions but it was obvious from the veins popping out the side of her neck that she was furious with the whole class. This kind of unrest while she was trying to teach us about Shakespeare's sonnets was more than she could handle.

Eventually the giggles subsided. And we moved on to . . .

Shall I compare thee to a summer's day?

STRANGER THAN FICTION

Turns out the bedwetting thing was true. Or so we think. How did it leak? (Pun fully intended.) Whoever stole Doofus's diary ripped out a section of it, photocopied it and stuck it up around the school.

> Hundo % gonna skip camp. wot if I slash the bed again? No way I'm lettin' nobody know about the pee sitch. I ain't stoopid, ay?

Oh man . . . this would be embarrassing for anyone, but for a guy who's always flexing and acting tough, this must be EXTRA embarrassing. Tenfold – with a cherry on top.

The fact that it wasn't posted on social media and was instead literally posted (with sticky tape) on walls and toilet doors around the school got me thinking. It's obviously been done by someone not so tech savvy. Someone old-school. I mean, who actually puts things up on walls anymore? What is this, 1995? There's also the risk factor. Sticking up posters in broad daylight is crazy risky. You could get busted so easily. Posting online is clearly the better option: it reaches a bigger audience and no one can hold you accountable because it can be done anonymously. That's why so many coward bullies do it that way – they hide behind their keyboards and linger in the shadows because they don't actually have the guts to step into the light and show their mean, ugly souls to the world.

Whoever did this is either ancient and unfamiliar with cyberbullying or they're being nice and didn't want to ruin Doofus completely. Didn't want to leave a digital trail that could be searched and found forever and ever and ever until the end of time. Going paper instead of digital meant that Rufus 'Pee-wee' Sherman could one day apply for a job and his boss wouldn't come across this unfortunate bedwetting fact when googling his name. So, I guess that's something he should be thankful for.

But here's the most amazing part. A post-it note stuck on top read:

LEAVE MUTE BOY ALONE OR MORE DIARY PAGES WILL BE POSTED!

This was a warning.

Somebody was doing this for Aria! It did cross my mind that maybe Aria himself had done it. But I quickly dismissed that idea. It's just not his style. Also, he wouldn't refer to himself as 'Mute Boy'. I felt a huge sense of relief for him, though. Surely the bullying would stop now. We could all get on with our lives without worrying about where and when Doofus Rufus would strike again.

I didn't want to jinx it, but the rest of the day went without incident. Doofus kept a low profile, and apart from some hushed sniggering in the corridors, everything else was respectably boring. No drama. No fights. No more shouting teachers with angry frowns. Finally, a moment's peace and serenity . . .

Aria → serenity

The Oxford Dictionary – which I like to read for pleasure – defines ‘serenity’ as ‘the state of being calm, peaceful, untroubled’.

Untroubled.

I am always chasing serenity. Sometimes, in difficult situations, I have no choice but to create it for myself. If serenity had a colour, it would be blue. Sky blue. And its sound would be silence.

There was definitely a feeling of serenity that swept over the school this afternoon, once the unfortunate wee-wee problem was revealed. Rufus stopped stalking me and I stopped looking over my shoulder. It was a huge relief. I wondered if he’d leave me alone from now on. I doubted it . . . but one could only hope.

BOMBSHELL

I ran straight home after school. Usually I linger, chat to Jaz, buy some good eats. Hot chips and pink milk. Healthy and delicious. *Shh*, I know. I'm being sarcastic.

But no faffing about today. Today, I grabbed my bag, my books and bolted home. I couldn't wait to see Dad.

We never know how long his **UP** mood is going to last, so we try to soak it all in when it's here. Live in the moment, as Mum says. Enjoy the ride, no matter what. I swear my mum was born with an extra chromosome. The P chromosome.

P FOR POSITIVITY.

She always sees the best in any situation.

Most people aren't very understanding of moods. Up or down. Or sideways, for that matter. They don't know that some people's minds play tricks on them.

Mum says that sometimes the chemicals in Dad's brain get outta whack. But it doesn't mean that he's not Dad. He's just a different version of Dad. For a little while.

But the mood forecast for today was sunny. Sunny with a chance of tears. There's always a chance of tears but we were looking at clear skies at the moment so I didn't want to waste a single minute. I wanted to bask in the sun.

Dad was cooking when I got home. Spag bol. He was wearing the too-small apron I made in Design/Tech and he'd spilled red sauce all over it. He was dipping his finger into the saucepan for a taste when I walked through the door. His face immediately lit up.

'My Hero!'

'Hi, Dad,' I said as I examined our messy kitchen. It looked like a bomb had hit it. He'd been chopping and slicing and dicing and cooking up a storm. 'Is Mum still at work?'

'Yes,' he said. 'She's probably sniffing someone's stinky feet as we speak!'

I noticed that there were four pots on the boil. Big pots. All of them filled to the brim with spaghetti sauce.

'Are we having guests for dinner, Dad? This is a lot of sauce.'

He told me that he was cooking up a big batch to freeze. Which sounds sensible, except that this was bigger than a big batch. It was a ginormous batch. It could feed 100 people. There was definitely no room in our freezer for all this sauce. Still, too much sauce is better than Sad-Dad so I shrugged and hugged him hello.

I looked over at Skye. She was sprawled on the floor, wearing a tutu on top of her uniform, eating Cheetos and watching some game show on the iPad. All pretty standard.

I helped Dad scoop sauce into dozens of Tupperware containers for freezing. We had a whole production line going. Like a factory. We chatted as we scooped. I had missed our chats.

Dad likes to talk about Shakespeare. And books. Stories of any kind, really. He's a word whiz – he teaches English Literature at university, so he's interested in all things literary. And stories about storytellers. Authors. Poets. Playwrights. He's obsessed with them all. The only part of the newspaper he ever reads is the 'Arts and Culture' section.

As I lifted a ladleful of sauce from a pot and began tipping it into a container, Dad told me that today he'd read about a boy at my school who had just won the national poetry prize. A refugee from Iran.

'Aria Hakimi. Do you know him?'

I spilt my ladle of sauce all over the benchtop.

MIND OFFICIALLY BLOWN

WHAT?!
Aria?

Who never, ever speaks . . . is a poet?

Almost as if he could see the fireworks going off in my mind, Dad casually corrected my thoughts. 'He's an *award-winning* poet.'

He's also a refugee from Iran? I had no idea. My head was spinning. Too much news for one day. First, I woke up to 'new mood' Dad. Then we found out that the school's geriatric bully still wets the bed. And now Dad's telling me that my friend, who can't ACTUALLY speak any ACTUAL words, is an ACTUAL poet?!

Dad cleaned up my big SPLAT of sauce from the bench and went to his study to bring me the newspaper. Yes, my dad still buys newspapers. He'll never scroll through his phone to read anything. He likes the feel of the big, double-page spread. He likes the ink on his fingers from turning the pages. He even likes the musty smell of it. Dad walked back into the room, excitedly flipping through the pages, trying to find the Arts section.

'Here it is!' He read me the headline. '"Young refugee scoops up poetry prize".' I snatched the paper from my dad. OMG, it was actually Aria. There was a photo of him under the article. He was smiling, holding his framed award and shaking hands with some old guy. Probably the mayor. Do we have a mayor? Anyway, I couldn't believe my eyes. Dad pretended to be annoyed by my snatching and snatched the paper back. He read it aloud.

'"Iranian refugee Aria Hakimi was forced to flee persecution when he was nine years old. Now living in Australia, Hakimi has turned his pain into poetry. The 12-year-old was awarded the prestigious *Think Ink* prize, a national prize for young writers, for his poem entitled 'I am love' . . ."'

I.
Am.
Love.

Talk about a 'big-feels' title! Dad kept reading: '". . . a moving poem about the struggles of finding your voice within a brutal, oppressive regime."'

Finding your voice? That was ironic. Is that the right word? I never know. Irony always trips me up.

The poem itself wasn't printed but Dad's face was beaming. He was so impressed. He tossed the paper onto the kitchen bench and exclaimed, 'What an incredible young fella!'

I told Dad that Jaz and I had become friends with Aria. 'He's kind of quirky – like us. And super nice, but he doesn't speak. Which is probably why Rufus Sherman has been making his life hell on wheels.'

'What do you mean he *doesn't speak*?' asked Dad. 'You mean, he doesn't speak *English*?'

'No. He doesn't speak, full stop. He's speechless. Mute. He has no words.'

'Well, he has *some* words,' Dad happily pointed out. 'And those words have just won him $1000 in prize money.'

'Wow! A cool K?' I couldn't believe it. That made Aria the richest kid I knew. I could barely process all this. Information overload. But some of the pieces of the Aria puzzle were starting to come together.

In a matter of minutes, he had gone from being the mysterious Mute Boy to an award-winning poet who was now seriously cashed up! I had to tell Jaz. I had to tell her or I would spontaneously combust. It couldn't wait until tomorrow. So, I left Dad with his saucy apron and his spag bol and his 50,000 Tupperware containers to call Jaz.

CAN I HANG UP NOW?

Jaz

Woah, woah, woahhhh! Back up the truck, Hero. What do you mean he's a poet? Are you nuts?

Me

I swear. On Groucho's life.

Groucho was Jaz's pet snake and she loved him way more than anyone should ever love a snake.

Jaz

This better not be a prank. You *know* how I feel about Groucho.

Me

Look up today's news! I'm not kidding. There's a whole article about the award and a big pic of Aria receiving his prize. He's a refugee from Iran!

Jaz

Well, paint me green and call me a pickle.

Jaz always says weird things like that. Sometimes I think she's an old woman trapped in a 12-year-old body. We talked for ages. Going over the same information again and again. Aria's a poet. And a refugee. Did I mention he's a poet? And a refugee?

We had so much more to uncover about Aria. So much digging to do. This was just the tip of the Aria iceberg.

I wanted to hang up and get back to Dad but as you know, Jaz is a talker. Very hard to stop her when she's on the talk-train. And right then, she was all aboard. Tootin' and hootin' and yap, yap, yapping. If only *she* had a mute button. We moved on from the topic of our award-winning poet friend to the suspicious growth that had appeared on Jaz's pinky toe.

Another thing you should know about Jaz is that she is a hypochondriac. Don't know what that means? Let me explain. Jaz is always, ALWAYS complaining about some ailment.

A SWOLLEN TOOTH.

AN ITCHY KIDNEY.

AN INVISIBLE RASH.

There's always something that has her all panicked and tied up in knots. Of course, she googles every miniscule symptom and always convinces herself that there's something catastrophically wrong.

We talked about her lumpy pinky toe for an eternity. Actually, she talked. I listened. Actually, I didn't even listen. I just made listening noises like 'mm-hmm', 'yeahhh', 'oh really?' while I did the crossword in the Arts section of the paper.

Sixteen across – What is a four-letter word for rabbit?

Jaz

What if it grows and grows till
my foot can't fit into my shoe anymore?
I'd be a proper freak show then.

Me

(In my head) Bunny? No, that's five
letters.

Jaz

What if it starts sprouting hairs? Thick, long, curly monsters. Hair, hair, everywhere!

Me

That's it! Hare!

Jaz

(Obviously confused) Are you *celebrating* my soon-to-be freakishly big, hairy toe?

Hare (not hair) – is a four-letter word for rabbit. Jaz had just helped me with the crossword, without even meaning to. But it was too hard to explain all that to her. That I'd been doing a crossword puzzle for half the time she'd been talking. Instead, I told her that I had to go fish Skye's Barbie out of the toilet (it wouldn't have been the first time Skye thought Barbie would enjoy a dip in the loo) and finally got off the phone.

Paranoia Strikes Doofus

The next day at school, as I was heading towards the oval for PE, I saw Aria a few steps ahead. 'Hey, Aria, wait up!' I shouted as I ran to catch up to him. I had so many questions about his poetry win, but before I had a chance to speak, we saw Doofus. And not like we'd ever seen him before. Something was definitely off. He was acting strange. Muttering things to himself. Aria threw me a confused look as we watched Doofus frantically rummage through people's bags. He was manic. Like a ferret or a weasel, digging for answers.

'Where is it? Where IS IT?' he mumbled desperately.

I guessed he was looking for his diary. He must've figured that if it wasn't Aria who'd stolen it, then somebody else had. But who? Who was humiliating him on this epic scale? We watched him from a distance, unzipping backpacks, throwing books out onto the ground, creating a huge mess. Papers were flying out of bags like water out of a fountain.

'Rufus!' shouted Bruno Barbaro, the Year 10 rugby captain. 'What are you doing? That's my bag!'

Bruno was the only kid in school who was bigger than Doofus. He was built like a tank and could easily flatten The Doof if he wanted to, but for some reason, even Bruno feared Rufus. It was ridiculous, but what can I say? That's high school. Not much about it makes sense. Certainly not the social order: who's feared, who's popular. Who's pitied, admired, loved or loathed. No one knows why some cruise through high school without a care and others suffer. There's no real science to it. It is what it is: a chaotic mess of kids just trying to get to the finish line.

The one thing that is certain, though, is this: the loudest mouth creates the greatest fear. The more obnoxious you are, the more people are scared of you, no matter your size or strength. I guess that's the way of the world. Some of these bullies transform into proper human beings eventually (with empathy and a conscience) but some commit to the gig long term. They stay mean, and sometimes get meaner. They go on to become head-kicking corporate honchos and even world leaders.

Normally Doofus would've responded to Bruno with something stupid like, 'Ya startin' sumfink, bro?' and been all up in his face. But not today. Today, the newly humiliated Pee-wee Sherman froze when Bruno called him out. He mumbled something and quickly began to collect the papers and books which were now strewn all over the ground.

'Sorry, man. I was just looking for sumfink,' he said.

I looked closely at Doofus. He seemed smaller today. Could he have shrunk overnight? He was hunched in on himself. Like a deflated ball. Trying to blend in and not take up all the space. He collected Bruno's books and put them back in his bag. Bruno gave Doofus a dirty look and snatched his bag out of his hands. By now a crowd had gathered, sniggering and whispering. Then someone called out . . .

'Good luck with the potty training, moron!'

Everyone burst out laughing. Rufus turned purple with embarrassment. Aria and I looked at each other. I could see in Aria's eyes that he truly felt bad for Doofus.

'Who said that?!' shouted Doofus. He lunged towards the crowd of kids like a wild dog. Everyone managed to dodge him. Aria and I were the last to move out of his way.

He narrowed his eyes when he saw Aria.

'I'm gonna get you, Mute Boy. This is all your fault!'

I wasn't sure why he was blaming Aria for this public humiliation. Perhaps he was just an easy target. A kid who never speaks. Scapegoat for everything. Or maybe he still thought Aria was the mastermind behind the wee posters. Either way, Aria was copping it again. I guess bullies don't need reasons to pick on their prey. They decide on a particular 'punching bag' and home in on them until they either achieve complete annihilation or they get bored. Whichever comes first.

Doofus swung his arm and pushed Aria onto the ground. Alfie Toogood, Doofus's number-one goon, leapt towards the action and yanked Doofus off Aria.

No one was expecting that! This was the first time I'd seen him do *anything* other than stand by Doofus like a lump of lard. 'Let's get outta here, Roof, before a teacher comes,' he said, dragging Doofus away.

I helped Aria up. Thankfully he wasn't hurt, just had a small scrape to the knee. He was dusting himself off when Bruno Barbaro approached us.

'You okay?' he asked.

Aria nodded.

'Don't take it personally. He's got beef with everyone.'

Aria nodded again.

'By the way, congrats on your win. That's mad, ay?'

Bruno held out his fist for Aria to bump. Aria's face lit up. Here was the captain of the rugby team, the biggest, buffest, sportiest guy in school, congratulating him on his poetry prize and holding out his fist.

Aria grinned and responded with a joyful . . .

BUMP.

Aria → *balal* with my friends

Sometimes I have flashbacks.

Sometimes one little thing – a word, a smell, a gesture – will transport me back in time.

Today it was the fist-bump from Bruno Barbaro.

Today's flashback didn't take me to a dark place. Not to the sound of sirens, or the Revolutionary Guards breaking into our neighbour's house or my mother gasping for air as she tried to cling to life.

That heartfelt fist-bump took me straight to the backstreets of Shiraz, where the sound of kids' laughter used to echo, echo, echo ... echo echo ec

Where I played soccer with my best friend Amir and the other kids in the neighbourhood. Too poor for smartphones or video games, we had simple pleasures. Kicking a ball. With makeshift goalposts. The grit and dirt from the unpaved road would get stuck in my sandals but I didn't care. All I wanted to do was score a goal and when I did . . . well, that was truly exhilarating! Hugs, cheers and fist-bumps were how we celebrated. Hassan, an oversized, overzealous kid from uptown, was the self-appointed coach, referee and commentator, all in one. He would always shout from the sidelines.

'Mashallah! Damet garm!'

He was larger than life. With a laugh to match. One of his many skills was that he could fart on cue. His nickname was Hassan Goozoo, which literally means 'Hassan the Farter'. Every time one of us scored a goal, he'd cheer, holler, then lift one leg into the air and let it rip!

Let it rip.

It's a funny expression. I like all the Aussie expressions for farting.

Cut the cheese.

Bum burp.

Release the beast.

Let one loose.

Australian kids appreciate a well-orchestrated fart. And I respect that. Hassan Goozoo would be very popular here.

We'd kick that football back and forth for hours and hours until the sun went down. We'd stop sometimes to let pedestrians pass. Or the odd motorbike. My mum would always come by with snacks to keep us going. Usually *balal* – roasted corn that she'd buy from the street vendors nearby. She'd never just buy one for me. She'd buy dozens so every kid got one. She didn't care who they were, or from which part of town. She loved them all. Even the showy, overconfident, flatulent ones like Hassan. She always spent what little money we had on others. That was her way.

Today, for some strange and wonderful reason, Bruno's fist-bump transported me to that happy place. Suddenly, I wasn't wiping blood off my knee after being shoved to the ground by the big idiot but instead, I was home . . . playing soccer and eating delicious, chargrilled *balal* with my friends.

DAGGY DANCE

Jaz does this thing when she's happy. I call it the 'Daggy Dance' but it's not really a dance. It's a whole lot of silly. She raises both arms in the air and clicks her fingers, making a *click, click, clickety-click* rhythmic sound. As her fingers are clicking, her butt is doing a hula hoop kind of twirl back and forth. Not a twerk. Please don't be imagining that. Think silly. Ultra-silly. Her hips look disconnected from her torso as she moves her bottom in a circular motion. Oh, and she cheers for herself as she's dancing. Lots of **chirping, cooing, woo-hooing** sounds. She's like a party bus on two legs. Jaz doesn't bust out the Daggy Dance often, but when she does, it lights everything up. Changes the temperature of the room to EXTREME joy. It's impossible to feel mad or sad when she pulls out the moves.

As soon as Jaz spotted Aria, she broke out into her

dance. It was just what Aria needed after yet another Doofus encounter. I think this must've been the first time he had witnessed the glory of the Jaz dance because at first, he froze.

She exploded with excitement. 'And the winner is . . .'

Unsure of what Jaz was so excited about, Aria looked around to see if he had missed something. But Jaz made a beeline straight for him, calling out . . .

'Ariaaaaa!'

She shoved a pretend mic into Aria's face.

'Tell us, Mr Hakimi, how long have you been a secret poetry-writing, prize-winning FREAKING legend?'

Aria finally caught on. He smiled. Small at first. All humble. Then he hung his head, looking a bit embarrassed.

'Oh, that's right. You don't speak. My apologies. Perhaps you could issue a press release? We're all dying to know more. Tell us everything!'

'Jaz!' I said, giving her a side-eye, which meant 'enough already'. She can really go too far sometimes. But no one was going to rein her in. No way. She was a whole mood. She continued with the dance. Her butt seemed to detach itself from her body entirely and do its own crazy thing around the schoolyard. Aria laughed.

When the spectacle was finally over, she caught her breath and placed both hands on Aria's shoulders.

'Yo, seriously though, why didn't you tell us you were a word whiz?'

He shrugged.

'Also, what are you doing with your fat stack of cash? Thousand bucks, right? 'Cause, you know, there's this new scooter I've had my eye on for a while.'

It sounded like Jaz was joking but I couldn't be sure. She's not shy when it comes to asking for things she wants. Like that time she asked for my favourite red beanie because she thought she was suffering from a rare medical condition which was giving her oversized goosebumps on her scalp. I tried to tell her that being cold wasn't a medical condition but she wouldn't listen. If I didn't give her my beanie pronto, she might be admitted to hospital with a severe case of bumpy-head-itis. Suffice it to say, that beanie is now hers.

Aria didn't seem to mind Jaz hitting him up for a new scooter. He just laughed. I think he was enjoying the fuss and attention.

Jaz, who wanted to know everything about Aria's poetry win, had brought her old Etch A Sketch to school just so she could communicate faster with him. She whipped it out of her bag and repeated her previous demand.

'TELL US EVERYTHING!'

Aria responded as you would imagine.

He did nothing.

Jaz shoved the board into his hands and continued with her questions.

'Can I read the poem?'

'What is it about?'

'How long have you been writing?'

'Let's talk about Iran. Where is that even?'

Aria threw me a comical look that said 'help!'. I threw him one back that said 'sorry, buddy, there's no stopping this freight train'.

Truth is, I was just as curious as Jaz. I'm just more polite about it. Less like a tornado. After 1001 questions from Jaz and a few scribbles on the Etch A Sketch from Aria, we found out a bit more.

Aria had always loved poetry. His mother introduced him to the famous Persian poet Rumi when he was just five years old. Aria used to write poems in Farsi. He still does. But also, now, in English.

He wrote down something that I'll never forget:

Words have power.

This coming from a boy who doesn't speak. Let's just think about that for a moment. If words have power, then was he powerless? Was poetry his way of reclaiming that power? And why do words have power anyway? They're just words, right? Blah, blah, blah . . .

This was a question for Dad. Word Nerd extraordinaire.

WORDS

Dad's UP mood escalated a hundredfold when I asked him about his thoughts on . . . words.

You have to understand, my dad's love of words isn't exactly normal. He used to read to me and Skye while we were still in Mum's tummy. And not just those alphabet picture books or *The Very Hungry Caterpillar*. He would read *The Lord of the Rings* and *The Magic Faraway Tree*. And he'd do all the voices. He'd act out the book to an unborn baby (probably with no ears yet) swimming in a sack of goo, inside Mum's stretched-out belly. I watched him do it night after night for Skye. Mum and I never questioned it. We loved listening to Dad do a live audiobook every night. You see what I mean? He loves words the way some people love dogs. Or burgers. Or roller-coasters.

He eats stories. Devours poetry and flosses his teeth with prose. If he could, he'd probably marry words.

So, he was exactly the right person to talk to about Aria and *his* love of words.

'I want to meet this Aria!' he exclaimed, his arms flailing in the air like an old Italian nonna greeting her grandchildren at the door. 'First of all, did you know that the name *Aria* means 'melody' in Italian, 'lioness' in Hebrew and 'noble' in Farsi, which is his language?'

I did not know that. No.

Dad continued. 'That kid is bang on, my Hero. Words *do* have power. If you just choose the right ones. And put them in the right order. And breathe a little bit of your soul into them, then you can create magic.'

Dad's excitement was escalating with each sentence. He was leaping about the room. Talking with passion, as if he were addressing a lecture theatre full of his eager English Literature students. I looked at Mum, who was relaxing into the couch and watching Dad with a smile. As always, I could read her face. She was one person who didn't need words. Her expression said it all: 'I love him. Thank you, universe, for lifting him out of his fog.'

Dad went on. He talked about how at certain times in his life, words had helped heal him. I mean, sure, he still needed doctors and medication and *meditation*, but words had helped heal a broken spirit. Or at least patch it together a bit.

'Have you ever been transported by a story, Hero?' asked Dad. I wanted to say yes, but the truth is that I'm not much of a reader. My eyelids get very heavy as soon as I pick up a book. Like they're being dragged down by bricks. The sentences start to blur into each other and my mind starts to wander. I guess I'm more of a Netflix person. Not that I'd ever admit that to Dad.

'Stories are an escape, an adventure! A place where we lose *and* find ourselves,' he said.

Once, during one of his DOWN periods, Dad read *The Lion, the Witch and the Wardrobe* and somehow, this story about an evil witch and talking animals helped him feel better about the world. Another time, he read a book called *The Book Thief* about a girl in Nazi Germany, also obsessed by the power of words, whose life was literally saved by reading and writing. He cried while he was reading that one but he said they were 'good tears'. The kind that make you want to be a better person.

So, yes, to him words were healing. They were medicine.

WORDS HAD POWER.

Dad kept talking, being very serious, but the whole time his mouth was moving, I couldn't help but think of silly words. Funny words. Rude words. They just kept popping into my head, uninvited. One after another. Words like . . .

Bruh.

Fungus.

Malarkey.

Swamp.

Gooey.

Flubber.

And the more I tried to push them out, the more they came flooding in. Little did Dad know that while he was delivering his monologue about the power of words –

'"To be or not to be: that is the question": you see what Hamlet is doing there? With just a few words, he's making us think about ALL of existence. Life and death. The whole shebang!'

– a whole bunch of silly words were elbowing their way into my headspace.

They were saying:

'Hey, don't forget about us. We're important too. Don't worry about Hamlet's big, fancy-pants words. *We* make you laugh. We make you squirm. We make you squeal with delight at the fact that we even exist! You sayin' the word "bumfuzzle" doesn't have power too? POWER to all bumfuzzles!'

The silly words were protesting. They were holding up signs and placards. They were chanting

'Sputnik!
Dung!
Bumbag!'

Okay, okay . . . I hear you, silly words. You are words too. And yes, all right, you deserve your own chapter.

Silly Words

Welcome to the chapter devoted to silly words. This is a happy place, as you will soon see. The words you're about to read won't be found in any Jane Austen novels. Or in Shakespeare's plays. Although, he had plenty of sillies in his work. But none like the ones that were creeping into my head. Here's a small sample of the wacky words that came raining into my mind as Dad was talking:

→ **SHIH TZU** – sounds rude, but it's not. A type of furball. Woof! Dog with short legs and floppy ears.

→ **DOPPELGANGER** – a twinsie who isn't actually your twin.

→ **NOODLE** – you know what it means. Say it over and over and over out loud. Are you doing it? Funny, right?

→ **PIE HOLE** – shut it or I'll shut it for you. Means 'mouth', for those not in the know.

- **MALTIPOO** – also a type of furball. Fluffy puppy. Cuteness level – off the chart.
- **LARD** – aka fat.
- **WEASEL** – stinky animal. Also, a sneaky human.
- **COLLYWOBBLES** – that urrgh feeling in your belly just before an exam.
- **NINCOMPOOP** – an idiot, a schmuck, Rufus Doofus.
- **ESPRESSO** – a type of coffee. Not a cappuccino, flat white or a latte with soy, almond, decaf, half-caf or mega-caf. Just another pretentious adult word for coffee.
- **GENUPHOBIA** – fear of knees.

I wondered if any of those words had power. If they changed lives. Probably not. Anyway . . .

Back to Dad

'We've got to help him enter more competitions. National. International. Intergalactic, even. There's no limit to what this kid can achieve!'

'Dad, chill! You can't enter him into writing competitions . . . here or in outer space. He doesn't even know you.'

'Well, that's an easy fix,' said Dad. 'Let's have him over for dinner.'

The way he saw it, Aria was his kindred spirit and it was his duty to help catapult him into a world of literary fame. Mum didn't think it was such a good idea for us to foist ourselves onto Aria. He probably didn't want a bunch of well-meaning folk suddenly acting as his agent. I agreed.

Plus, it would be weird to have him over for dinner. For starters, he didn't speak. And considering Dad's current mood, Dad probably wouldn't STOP speaking!

It would be a one-way word tunnel that would leave Aria gasping for air.

But Dad was not taking no for an answer. He was already deciding on the menu. 'Invite his parents too. And Jaz! I'll make some more spaghetti Bolognese.'

'NO!' Mum and I said (a little too loudly) at the same time. Then we all burst out laughing. 'We have enough spag bol to last us till next century!' said Mum.

Skye, who was doing an open-door number two (that's pooing with the toilet door wide open for those not in the know), added her voice to the discussion. 'No more pasgetti!'

This made Dad laugh. 'Okay, fine. How about tacos? Did somebody say "Taco Tuesdaaaaay"?'

I guess Aria was coming to dinner because we were now discussing cuisine details. The thing is that Dad believed in Aria. Here was a kid with stories to tell. It didn't matter that he was mute. He had now found his voice. And we had to help him amplify it. Mum and I knew that when Dad got fixated on something he believed in, especially when he was in an UP mood, there was no stopping him. So, we decided to invite Aria and his parents to our house for dinner.

I started thinking that maybe this wasn't the worst

idea in the world. Aria was my friend. And friends have friends over, right? Also, the nosy side of me who was still trying to piece together the Aria puzzle was keen to find out more about his family. And his home. And the escape from that home.

Aria himself was a story . . . wrapped in a story.

I guess we all are.

Not-Miserable Ms Rubble

Ms Rubble was not miserable today. No. Today she was elated. That's a fancy word for happy. What do you think was making her happy?

* Beating her own personal record of handing out detentions – 407 in one day.
* Discovering a device that would electrocute late-comers as they entered her class.
* Travelling back in time to when it was still legal to poke kids with a sharp stick if they forgot to do their homework.

Good guesses, but it was actually none of the above. Ms Rubble was happy because of Aria. She had read the article about him winning the poetry prize and was overjoyed that among this bunch of tardy, annoying, sloppy students, there was also a poet. And an award-winning one at that. Aria wasn't even in *her* English class. He did ESL (English as a second language) with

Mr Fig. But she was boasting about him like he was not only her student, but her own child.

'What a marvellous young man!' she exclaimed, sounding like my dad. 'This boy came to this country without a word of English and is now writing poetry. Poetry!'

As she paced the room and praised Aria, her happy tone started to turn to a frustrated one. At us. For not being as clever as Aria. She put her hands on Jaz's desk and towered above her. 'If he can write poetry, what's your excuse for this dog's breakfast? There are 500 spelling mistakes on every line!'

She plonked Jaz's comprehension test in front of her. Big red marks all through it. Poor Jaz. She wasn't the world's best speller. But who was?

Aria, apparently.

Ms Rubble continued. If we could all just learn from Aria, take a chapter out of his book, blah, blah, blah . . .

She said Jaz had to go to the Faculty Room at lunch and write out the dictionary from A to Z.

'You're kidding, right, Ms Rubble?'

Ms Rubble leant right in again, the shadow of her head looming above Jaz like a dark, ominous cloud.

'Do I LOOK like I'm kidding, Jasmin?'

Jaz gulped. No, she wasn't kidding. Ms Rubble doesn't kid. She's no joker. This was serious business.

'There's a lot of rude words in the dictionary, Ms Rubble,' said Jaz. 'Some of them starting with the letter "F" . . . and, I dunno, "S" . . . Do I write them ALL down?'

Ms Rubble's eyes widened with horror. Her nostrils flared. Smoke started coming out of her ears. I thought she might pull out an axe from her back pocket and slice Jaz's desk in half.

'Never mind, Ms Rubble,' said Jaz smoothly. 'Don't answer that. I'll just skip the rudies. Don't want to pollute my mind . . . or yours. 'Cause of course, you'll be marking my handwritten dictionary, right?'

I threw Jaz a look – **SHUT YOUR PIE HOLE ALREADY!**

Jaz just grinned at me. The girl is fearless. Ms Rubble took a deeeeeeeeep breath, clenched her fists and closed her eyes. She looked like she wanted to murder Jaz but that would definitely get her fired. So, instead, she exhaled and told Jaz that she'd see her in the Faculty Room at lunchtime.

As Ms Rubble clicked her shoes together and turned on her heels, Jaz leant into me and whispered, 'Holy Moses, how am I going to get out of this one?'

In the closet

Lunchtime rolled around. Jaz dragged me through the yard till we found Aria. She had decided that we would retreat to the janitor's closet for the duration of lunch. That was the safest place. Ms Rubble would never find her there.

Aria was happy about this retreat too. It was a good hide-out from Doofus.

We squished ourselves among the brooms, mops and a whole lot of cleaning chemicals. It was pretty gross but breathing in all the toxic fumes seemed like a fair price to pay if the alternative was spelling detention and more Doofus encounters.

We sat cross-legged on the floor, our knees touching. Jaz had brought a deck of cards to school so I decided to teach my friends how to play poker. Jaz had only seen poker played in movies, so she decided to take on a persona. She was no longer

Jaz. She was Donna Corleone – Mafia Goddess. Her mouth curled into an upside-down smile and her voice became throaty. She scratched under her chin like a smooth operator, the big boss playing poker with her goons. And she spoke with the perfect Italian–American Noo Yawk accent.

'You in or out, Shorty?'

'You talkin' to me?' I asked in the worst New York accent ever. By now, we were all getting into the Mafia mood. 'And who you callin' shorty, Shorty?'

I lengthened my neck and glared down at Jaz who was definitely shorter than me. Jaz and Aria laughed at my terrible Godfather impersonation. I kept a straight face. Took a deep breath. Gave them both the stink-eye and said, 'I'm in,' all the while making sure I kept my cards close to my chest.

Jaz did a pretend evil laugh, 'Mwahahahah,' and confidently plonked down her cards. 'Read 'em and weep, suckas,' she said triumphantly, as if she'd just won the biggest hand ever played in the history of poker.

Except there was a teeny problem. Jaz didn't really know how to play poker. She clearly wasn't listening when I explained the rules. She's not big on rules at the best of times. I looked at her hand.

A pair of eights.

The. Worst. Hand. Ever.

She'd lost by a mile but she grinned and rubbed her Mafia belly and declared herself the winner. There was no arguing with her. Winning was a state of mind with Jaz. Aria was happy to fold. He threw down his cards but I happily displayed mine because I had two pairs. And even though that's a crummy hand, two pairs still beats one pair.

'Are you messin' wit me, Hero?'

'Umm . . .'

'Nobody messes wit me. Ya hear me? NOBODY!'

She actually scared me a little. For a millisecond, nobody said anything. Then I burst out laughing. So did Aria. Jaz always knew how to make us laugh. That was her secret weapon.

And after being shoved to the ground by Doofus yesterday, laughter was just the kind of healing medicine Aria needed.

Aria → midnight run

I've been to three different schools in my life. One in Iran and two in Australia. Rufus is not unique to this school. Mean kids exist everywhere. I try not to focus on them too much. My mother taught me to always focus on the good around me. To never let hate in. 'Hate clogs the arteries of the heart,' she used to say. 'It pollutes the membranes. It has no place there, Aria. Like an intruder into a sacred place.'

If I could speak at school, I'd say . . . *thank you* to Jaz and Hero.

Thank you for seeing me.

And for hearing me – even though I have no voice.

I'd say thank you for making me laugh.

I'd tell them stories about my life.

My life before this life.

My life in Iran.

I'd tell them that when I was nine years old, I lived

in Shiraz, a beautiful city in the south of the country. We didn't have much but I was happy. One night, as my brother Samir and I were finally dozing off to sleep in our bunk beds (we'd always get to sleep late because we couldn't stop talking and telling each other stupid jokes), there was a desperate knock on our bedroom window.

My heart almost stopped. Samir sat up with a fright. So did I. Did we imagine that? Surely, no one could be knocking on our window. We lived in an apartment, on the second floor. How could anyone have made it to our balcony window without coming through the house?

THUD!
THUD!

Okay, definitely didn't imagine that. Samir jumped out of bed and ran to get Maman and Baba. I hugged my knees and cried.

THUD!
THUD!
THUD!

Our parents came rushing in. Baba went to the window and opened the curtains. It was our next-door

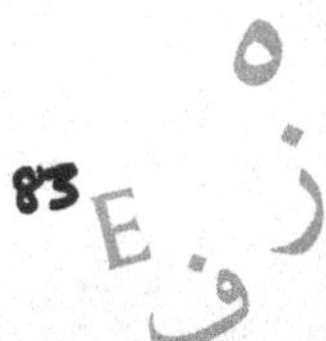

neighbour, Jamal. He had somehow managed to jump from his balcony onto ours. He had come to warn us. The Revolutionary Guards had come to his house – the wrong house by mistake – looking for my mother.

Maman.

They were looking for her.

Jamal had quickly realised what was going on when he heard his wife answer the door. He frantically grabbed whatever cash he had in his wallet, and, still in his pyjamas, made the three-metre jump across from his balcony to ours. It was a mighty jump. He didn't really stop to think it through before taking the leap. He could easily have fallen and broken every bone in his body. But he was a dear friend and he knew that if they found Maman, we'd never see her again.

You see, some officials in the government found my mother problematic. She refused to wear the hijab. She fought for women's rights. She spoke up against the injustice of the regime. She had a blog. It had six million followers. She was too outspoken. Had too much of a voice. My mother was definitely *not* mute.

They wanted her.

They wanted her *dead*.

We didn't stop to think. In that panic-stricken whirlwind of a moment, we grabbed our coats, shoes and Jamal's money and snuck quietly out the back fire escape, ran through several alleyways and finally hailed a taxi to take us to my grandmother's house a few suburbs away.

I never saw my house again after that night.

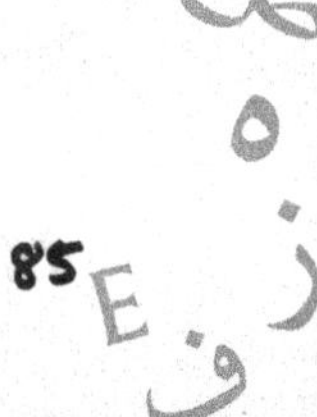

Dear Diary . . .

Jaz ended up with two detentions for failing to write out the entire dictionary. She thought that was a good deal. The next day, as I walked into school, I saw another note – stuck to the gate. It read . . .

> Aced me geoprafy assinement & it only cost me $20. Winning!

It was another page, photocopied from Doofus's diary. Copied multiple times and stuck everywhere around the school. On the noticeboard. Next to the canteen 'specials'. At the school bus stop. Everywhere. This new revelation would get Rufus into big trouble with his teachers. Ms Rubble would roast him on a spit and feed him to the staff for Christmas lunch!

Turned out he paid the smart kids in his year to do his assignments. Twenty dollars isn't much but it probably came with a threat of flushing their heads down the loo if they didn't oblige. I dread to think how many poor kids had to sit up late doing his homework for him. These diary pages were exposing Doofus big time. Who was doing this? I wondered. I mean, everybody hated Doofus – except for Alfie Toogood and the other nameless thugs who were his mates. But who would have the guts to take him on like this? Of course, like last time, there was another post-it note stuck on top of the diary entry. Another warning . . .

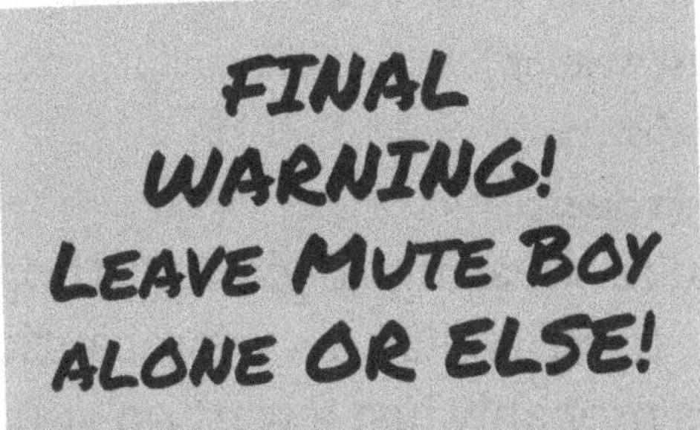

Maybe it really *was* Aria who was doing this? Just because he didn't speak didn't mean he couldn't plot a brilliant, wicked revenge.

Then Jaz showed up. Wearing a MOON BOOT. 'Have you seen 'em? They're everywhere! I just saw one on the back of the girls' toilet door!'

I didn't really hear what she said because I was so distracted by her giant shoe.

'Um . . . hello . . . Bigfoot?' I said casually.

'Remember the growth on my pinky toe?' she said.

'Yeah . . .?'

'Remember how I was worried about it growing big and then bigger and then getting totally out of control?'

'Jaz, why are you wearing a moon boot? Have you really got a ginormous growth on your pinky that requires a space outfit?'

'Well . . . no. Not exactly,' she said. 'But I found my mum's old boot from when she had her skiing accident, so I'm just wearing it as a precaution.'

'Say what, now?'

'Just in case.'

'You're wearing a giant orthopaedic device to SCHOOL as a precaution for what is probably just a wart on your little toe? Is this really what you're telling me?'

'No, Hero. I'm telling you that Doofus's diary pages

are plastered all over the school again. My big foot is a side issue. Stop deflecting.'

I loved the fact that Jaz didn't even care about what she looked like wearing the boot. Jaz doesn't care one little bit about what people think. She's the most self-assured paranoid hypochondriac I know.

After we moved on from the moon boot and went back to talking about the posters, I started to get a little suss. Maybe Jaz was behind the diary revelations? Aria wouldn't go into the girls' toilets and stick posters behind the doors. It must be a girl. And what girl has a better motive than Jaz? She and I are Aria's best friends and I know that it wasn't me. So, it *must* be her.

But why wouldn't she tell me? She tells me everything. Too much, in fact. She tells me more than I ever really want to know. Hairy swollen pinky toe: case in point.

I decided to ask her straight out.

'Jaz, tell me the truth – did you steal Doofy's diary?'

She laughed in my face. As if I'd just told her the world's funniest joke.

HAHAHAHAHAHAHAHA

Laughter wasn't the answer I was looking for. I narrowed my eyes.

'So, I guess that's a no? You're not the diary bandit?' I asked. She kept laughing.

'Hero, you're totally deranged!' said the girl wearing a moon boot to school unnecessarily. 'As if I would go undercover in such a serious operation and not even tell you about it!'

Hmm, her denial was a little forced. So was the laughing. I was definitely suss. But if it wasn't Jaz, then who? Who else was so invested in Aria's wellbeing? Who else even cared?

DODGING THE DOOF

I was passing the library when I saw him. Rufus-Doofus-Sherman. Sitting on a bench, picking a bit of food from his hair. He smelt it. Screwed up his face and flicked it away. Then he sprawled himself across the bench and began to pick his nose.

A little pick at first. Looking from left to right, making sure no one was watching. I ducked behind a tree, unseen. Once the coast was clear, Doofus went to town on his nose.

Pick, pick, pick.

He was excavating that honker like his life depended on it. He inspected his finger. Ah, he'd got a good one. He then proceeded to make it into a ball with his fingers. He was about to flick it when he spotted me, trying to blend into the tree. He extended his boogery index finger.

'You want some?'

Seriously? Did he just . . .? Never mind. I started walking away, trying to escape the nose-picking oaf as quickly as possible. He called out to me.

'Oi, can I talk to you?'

I didn't respond. It's not wise to respond to The Doof. Only bad can come from it. Problem is, he doesn't care if you're listening, interested or not. He just talks AT you. So, he continued.

'Tell your mute mate to meet me in the library at lunch, okay?'

I sighed. Now we had to avoid the library too? It was actually one of the hide-outs we enjoyed the most because it was guaranteed to be Doofus-free. He's never there. I don't even think he can read.

'I'm not gonna hurt him. I just wanna talk to him, okay?'

I picked up pace and walked extra fast to my next lesson, texting Aria and Jaz on the way on our group chat.

Doofus alert! Avoid library at lunch.

Jaz was the first to reply.

Closet or the oval?

Science block? I wrote.

Aria chimed in.

See you there!

When the bell went, the three of us assembled behind the Science block. Almost at the same time. Like eagles landing, flying in from our previous posts.

A sigh of relief. Doofus wasn't going to find us here. He was probably lost in the Self-Help section of the library. Aria cracked open his lunch box and offered us some Persian baklava. It smelt amazing. He always packed extra eats for Jaz and me these days. Especially sweet eats. He knew how much we loved them. Jaz rejoiced and grabbed the biggest piece with both hands.

'Ah, thank you, my excellent friend!'

PULLED BY THE COLLAR

Aria was literally mid-bite when he was lifted into the air. Yanked by his collar by none other than the bully-in-chief – His Royal Thug-ness, Rufus Doofus Shmuckington.

'Didn't your little girlfriend here tell ya to come to the library? You left me hangin', Mute Boy.'

I hung my head. Here we go. Aria was about to cop it again and I was about to be a bystander – again. He dragged Aria to his feet. Threw an arm around his neck and guided him away. Jaz jumped up too. For the first time ever, she stood up to Doofus.

'Leave him alone, Rufus! What's he ever done to you?'

I couldn't believe it. Where had she found the courage? I was so proud. Doofus's eyes widened, like he couldn't quite believe she was talking to him.

'Ooh, what do we have here? Bit of a hero, ay?'

'No, *she's* Hero,' Jaz said, pointing at me. 'I'm Jaz!'

Doofus looked genuinely confused. His brain seemed to do a backflip as he tried to process what she had just said. Hero? Jaz? Were these actual names? To be fair, it *did* sound confusing. All he could muster in response was . . . 'Huh?'

He then tightened his grip around Aria's neck and pulled him in really close.

'Listen, mate, I know you're the one rippin' up me diary pages and stickin' 'em everywhere.'

Aria shook his head. It wasn't him.

'Or you've put somebody up to it. Gettin' someone to do ya dirty work.'

Aria shook his head again. Nope.

'I'll make you a deal. I'll give you twenty bucks, you get the diary back to me and this'll all be over.'

Aria shook his head a third time.

'All right, all right, thirty bucks.'

Aria tried to walk away but Doofus wasn't about to let him go. He yanked him back by the neck again.

'Fitty bucks! Come on, man. That's a lot of dosh. What do ya say, we have a deal?'

Aria tried to dislodge himself from Doofus's grip. He looked exasperated. Annoyed even. With more determination than I've ever seen him display before, Aria untangled himself from the clutches of evil and began to walk away.

That's when Doofus pounced. Before I knew it, he had Aria pinned to the ground, his knees crushing Aria's elbows into the cement. It looked like he was really going to hurt him this time.

Aria started crying. My heart was racing. I had to do something. I couldn't stand by anymore. Jaz must've been thinking the same thing because as soon as she saw the tears, she leapt onto Doofus's back, moon boot and all, and wrapped her arms around his neck. She looked positively puny next to him. Like an ant taking on an elephant. Doofus simply flicked her off his back. She went flying. Landed with a thud on the grass nearby. I could not believe it. One minute we're eating Persian baklava, the next we're in a full-blown rumble. Well, by 'we', I mean Jaz, Doofus and Aria.

Not me.

I stood, frozen. Heart pounding out of my chest. Watching in horror. I wanted to help but I couldn't move. Why couldn't I move? I'm sure you've heard of the 'fight or flight response' – how people respond in stressful, dangerous situations? They either roll up their sleeves and charge like a bull (as Jaz was bravely demonstrating) or they run for the hills. I don't fall into either category. My response is always the lesser-known *freeze* response. It's not logical. Nor is it a choice. Clearly, standing like a statue in the midst of all that chaos wasn't helping anyone. But it's all I could do. Doing *nothing* was once again all I could do.

After a few moments, Jaz picked herself up and charged towards Doofus again. I've never seen her so mad. She was pulling his hair and throwing punches (mostly into the air because she's a bit un-co).

Jaz:

LEAVE HIM ALONE, YOU MAGGOT!

Seeing Jaz turn into Dwayne 'The Rock' Johnson had a crazy, unexpected effect on me. It felt like an electric shock ran through every part of my body. I suddenly felt alive. For the first time ever, I snapped out of my frozen bystander mode and sprang into action. Before I knew it I, too, was trying to yank Doofus off Aria. Jaz and I descended on him like a couple of swooping magpies. But Doofus, being significantly older and larger than us, barely noticed our attack. He peeled us off his body as if he were picking off a couple of scabs. No force required.

Meanwhile, Aria was still pinned to the ground.

'I need that diary back, ya little turd. Please! I'll do anything.'

'HE DOESN'T HAVE IT, YOU OVERGROWN BRAINLESS BULLY!' shouted Jaz.

Alfie Toogood suddenly appeared. He had a habit of doing that. Just materialising. Like a hologram. He must've heard Jaz shouting and come running. Toogood looked agitated, almost panicked – which was weird. His reactions lately were definitely strange. He wasn't piling on and acting like a butthead as you'd expect – but he wasn't exactly objecting to the bullying either. He was a hard one to decode.

Just as I was speculating about the inner workings of Alfie's pea-sized brain, I saw him take out his phone and snap a pic of Doofus pinning Aria to the ground. Or was he filming? I wasn't sure. After a few moments, Doofus looked up – angry.

'What the hell are ya doing, man?'

'Ah, nuffin . . . I mean, just taking a funny pic, ay? Of you flattenin' the kid. You still got it, Roof. Full strength, bruh.'

Doofus smiled. Puffed out his chest. He may have been suffering humiliation in the eyes of the rest of the school but he was pleased that his chief goon still worshipped him. He finally let Aria go. Aria sat up and wiped his face. Jaz and I caught our breath and decided to cease fire, for now. Doofus straightened Aria's crumpled-up shirt and talked to him in a desperate, pleading way.

'All you gotta do is bring me the diary. I promise to give you money for it. Then we're sweet. Okay? No more hassles.'

Alfie swung his arm around his mate and dragged him away from the scene. Seeing the back of him was a relief. For now.

Aria → *taarof*

I feel bad for Rufus. He must be struggling if he's offering me bribe money for his diary. What he doesn't know is that I could never accept bribe money. Or any other kind of money. I almost didn't accept my poetry prize money.

Why? Because . . . *taarof*.

Taarof is a Persian word with no English equivalent. I guess you could call it 'good manners' taken to the extreme. To accept money from anyone for any reason isn't considered polite. And *taarof* requires one to be extra polite, extra generous, extra humble. Half the time we aren't even genuine about it but it's an expected cultural norm. *Taarof* is ingrained into us Iranians. It's in our DNA. We fight for the lower hand. Always offering what we have (and what we don't have) to others. It's shameful to be the taker in our culture. You must never be the taker. You must be the giver at all costs. Sometimes *taarof* can actually turn into a battle between Persians. A very polite battle, but a battle nonetheless. No one wants to be the one who backs down. If *taarof* were an Olympic sport, Iranians would win gold every time.

I remember back in Shiraz, the simple act of going to a restaurant with my relatives was a big deal. My *amoo* (uncle) would always reach for the bill before we'd even finished eating. Baba would then try to wrestle him for it, but would often lose. As the years went on, Baba learnt different tricks to beat Amoo to the bill. He'd secretly hand his credit card over to the waiter before we even sat down. This worked a couple of times. Then my *amoo* caught on and would call the restaurant a week before and give them his credit card details over the phone. My father was furious – ever so politely furious – when he discovered this. One time, he offered the waiter a huge tip to take his credit card instead of Amoo's. The poor waiter was caught in the middle. But he had to decline. *Taarof* has very specific rules. And all Persians understand them. You don't take someone's *taarof* triumph away from them. Not even for a handsome tip!

One of the many unwritten rules of *taarof* is that you never, EVER accept money from your children. So it was excruciatingly difficult for Baba to accept my prize money when I offered it to him. He went into full battle mode. Told me there was no way he would take it, that he didn't want it, didn't need it – but I know when he's lying. His ears turn red, like tomatoes. I know that Baba has been struggling to pay our bills. Even though he works two jobs, it's still hard for him to make ends meet. His whole life is devoted to me and Samir now. He works for us. He lives for us.

I'm proud to announce that I won my first ever *taarof* battle at the age of twelve and a half.

Baba accepted the money.

It felt good to help. And I know Maman would've been pleased.

GUESS WHO'S COMING TO DINNER?

Aria's dad couldn't come to dinner. When Mum called to invite them, he was apparently overjoyed. He apologised for not being able to come (he works a night shift most nights) but he said that Aria would be delighted to come with his older brother Samir. Hmm, I thought. Aria has a brother. Another piece of the puzzle collected. But Mum said that there was no mention of Aria's mother.

Mum, being discreet and polite, didn't probe too much, but she assumed they were probably divorced. Or maybe Aria's mum had passed away? Or she was still back in Iran? Either way, it was only Aria and Samir who showed up that night. Oh, and Jaz, of course. But she's often at my house so that was nothing unusual.

It was surprisingly not-weird to have Aria and Samir over for dinner. It was actually really nice. All eight of us squished around the dinner table like one big family.

Yes eight, if you count Thelma, Skye's imaginary friend who always has a place at the table.

Samir, who is almost 17, was so friendly and chatty. Chatty! The opposite of Aria. His English was good but he had a slight accent. He boasted about Aria's writing talents. Dad was so interested in everything he had to say. Aria seemed amused by it all. Of course, he didn't speak, but it was the most relaxed I'd ever seen him. He ate Dad's tacos with gusto, giving Dad a literal thumbs-up after his first mouthful. Dad was over the moon. Taco Tuesday was off to a good start!

During dinner, my parents talked to Samir but were careful not to ask any questions that might be triggering for him. About the family's escape, especially. Or where the boys' mother was. Samir spoke about their life back in Iran. About how hard it was for them to leave their friends and family behind. He told us that after fleeing Iran, they had lived in Pakistan for a while.

'Boy, you really get around, kid,' said Jaz, sounding like a nana again. She's the only kid I know who calls other kids 'kid'. As if she's so much older and wiser. Neither of which she is.

Samir smiled and told us that both he and Aria spoke Urdu.

'You speak . . . what, now?' asked Jaz

'Urdu is the national language of Pakistan, Jaz,' said Dad.

I thought that was a strange thing for Samir to say. Clearly Aria didn't *speak* Urdu because he doesn't speak. But I guess he meant that Aria *understood* it. Which was still impressive.

We moved from Samir's sweet recollections of Iran – the neighbourhood kids having snow fights on the streets in winter; drinking the sour juice of a pomegranate straight from the pierced fruit itself; jumping over bonfires during their festive season – onto other things.

Jaz things.

She had us all in fits of laughter as she told us about her latest medical affliction – 'Alice in Wonderland Syndrome'. It was a perception disorder. No, she didn't make it up and no, we weren't allowed to laugh.

'Sometimes I see things really, REALLY small. Like, last week, I looked over in class and your head was the size of a pea, Hero. Literally a pea,' she said without blinking. I touched my head self-consciously. She continued, 'You had this incy-wincy speck of a head but a HUGE body. Massive. Guns like John Cena.'

As usual, Jaz was being overly dramatic. Which made it even funnier. We couldn't help but laugh, despite her strict instructions not to. Dad was the only one who held it together. He consoled Jaz and reassured her that her condition would pass.

This dinner had turned out much better than I had anticipated. Dad was at his best. Lively. Happy. Interested in everything and everyone. Feeding us endless tacos and cracking some of his classic, very lame dad jokes, which Jaz and Aria seemed to genuinely enjoy. I looked around the room at everyone talking, eating, being cheery, and my heart expanded. It felt like someone had inserted a pump into it and blown it up to triple its size. That heart-burst feeling is the same feeling I get when I see Dad lift out of his fog.

I felt so much love for my family at that moment. For my dad, whose kindness always shines through. For my mum, who is made of steel. She really is a warrior. And even Skye, who had somehow managed to sit through dinner without picking her nose, even once. Nor did she have full-blown conversations with Thelma, like she usually does. It was a miracle dinner.

After we'd finished clearing away the plates, Dad presented Aria with a big, long list of the various competitions he could enter next.

'All right, young man, let's have a look at what's out there.'

He plonked a bunch of newspaper clippings, magazine articles and entry forms onto the table.

'So many opportunities. We've got . . . the Alphabet Soup comp. The Right to Write – Young Writers comp. The Kids' Poetry Club comp.'

Aria flicked through the clippings, looking amazed. There were so many competitions he could enter. So many prizes to be won. He could even get published in kids' magazines, online publications or poetry anthologies. It's a shame he couldn't speak, because if he could, then he could enter the slam poetry comp that had the biggest prize of all: a trip for the winner and their family to Scotland to perform the winning poem at the Fringe Festival in Edinburgh!

'Sorry, mate. I shouldn't have thrown that one into the mix,' said Dad, retrieving the entry form from the pile. Samir asked what 'slam poetry' meant. Dad explained. 'It's kind of a cross between reciting and rapping. It's performance poetry. Usually in front of a crowd. Usually about a topic that is close to the poet's heart.'

Samir was captivated. 'Can you please tell me more?' he said.

Dad elaborated: 'I've been to a few Open Slam nights – they can be hit and miss but when someone nails it, it's very powerful. The atmosphere becomes electric. Raw. It stirs up the crowd and they get involved. It's amazing, actually.'

Samir looked to Aria as if to say, 'How about it?' I don't know why he was putting him on the spot like that. Slam poetry was clearly not an option. You can't enter a contest like that if you have no voice!

Aria went into a momentary trance. His body was there, slouching into our worn-out armchair, but his mind was elsewhere. You could see thoughts racing through his head, crashing into each other. He looked at Samir. Samir looked at Aria. What were these two brothers talking about without even opening their mouths?

And then it happened.

Aria spoke.

'I'll do it,' he said. 'I'll enter.'

Jaz LITERALLY fell off her chair. My jaw fell to the floor (not literally). Mum and Dad looked at each other in disbelief.

Aria was not mute.

Aria could speak.

Aria → it's complicated

You already know that I can speak. I can speak at home. I can speak with my therapist. But I am physically unable to speak at school. Cannot utter a word. It's a hard feeling to describe. It's not that I *choose* not to speak at school. I simply can't. I freeze at the very thought of it. It feels like my mouth has been stapled shut or suddenly filled with cement. Even if I could open my mouth, there's no sound. As though someone has stolen my voice box. Reached right down into my throat and unplugged all the wires. Pulled them out. If I try to fight it, to find my voice, my heart begins to race. I feel panicked. My head begins to spin clockwise, then anticlockwise, and back again until everything is a blur and I can't see straight. So, I don't speak at all. It's much easier that way. I let the noise and chaos of school wash over me like a wave.

I haven't always been like this. If you ask Amir or any of my friends back home, they'll tell you I'm a talker. Well, I *was* a talker. I'm working hard on overcoming this 'Mute Boy' problem. I know it doesn't seem like I'm making much progress but tonight I spoke in front of everyone at Hero's house. And even crazier, I made a pledge to enter a slam poetry competition.

I cannot believe I did that. Impossible task. Insurmountable mountain.

What was I thinking?

Holy Guacamole!

'Well, cut me in half and call me Shorty!' said Jaz once she picked herself up off the floor. 'I knew it! I knew you could talk!' She turned to me, bursting with excitement. 'Didn't I tell you that he was pranking us all?'

Samir explained that Aria wasn't pranking anyone. That he suffers from an anxiety problem that developed after they left Iran. But it isn't permanent. He will be okay one day. Hopefully soon. He thought it would be good for Aria to enter the slam poetry comp. It would be good for his confidence, a goal he could work towards with the support of his wonderful friends – us!

Dad jumped in. He said that he understood how Aria must be feeling. Of course, not *exactly*, because he would never be able to understand what it feels like to be forced to leave your homeland, learn a new language and start a new life, but he knew what it felt like to be anxious. To not cope. To shut down. Aria listened. He didn't say any more words that night but he seemed comforted by what Dad was saying.

Halfway through Dad and Aria's bonding moment, Jaz whispered to me, 'Dude, while I fully appreciate today's episode of "Therapy with Dr Rodriguez", can you puh-leaaaase stop all this "feeling" talk? I'm breaking out in a rash!'

Jaz was not big on serious conversations. Especially ones about feelings. It made her uncomfortable. I get that. Big-feels talks are not for everyone. I'm used to them because of my dad. My family has always been open. We talk about everything. The UPs, the DOWNs and the in-betweens. Nothing is off the table for us. And even though I could see that Aria was pleased about my dad's support, I knew that I had to change the mood for Jaz's sake. So, I stood up and made an announcement.

'Who wants dessert?'

Everyone's hands shot up. Skye unplugged herself from her *PAW Patrol* episode and squealed. 'ICE-CREAM!'

Aria → one day I will tell them . . .

Being with Hero's family was wonderful. I only said a few words but I could have said more. I felt like I could tell them anything. Things I've never told anyone. About our escape. About my mother. About that fateful day at my old school which changed the course of my life forever. But they were all so shocked to hear me speak (shocked in a good way, but shocked nonetheless) that I thought I'd wait.

When the time is right, I will tell them. I will tell them about the time the Revolutionary Guards came to my school in Shiraz . . . looking for me.

Since our narrow escape to my grandmother's house a few nights before, they'd redoubled their efforts to find my mother. But they couldn't find her anywhere. They went to our neighbours' homes. Nearby hotels. And eventually my grandparents' house. But by then, we had moved on. Maman's best friend Leila had insisted that we hide at her place. It was the safest option. They wouldn't know to look for her there.

Maman did some *taarof* at first, not wanting to burden her friend, but common sense trumped *taarof* this time. In this instance, Leila's kindness literally saved Maman's life. My parents both took some time off work to figure out what to do next. Would we move to Tehran and lose ourselves in the big city? Or perhaps we'd go to Isfahan, a beautiful town north of Shiraz.

Despite the chaos and uncertainty, my parents wanted life to remain as normal as possible for me and Samir, so we continued going to school. They figured we'd be safe there.

They were wrong.

The Revolutionary Guards showed up at my school at 12.43 pm on Friday 4 June. They had come to take me and hold me for ransom. Yes, they came to kidnap me. That must sound unbelievable to you. The thought that someone could just show up at your school and, at gunpoint, demand to take you away. It's like some kind of nightmare. Or a horror movie. Except that this was exactly what happened.

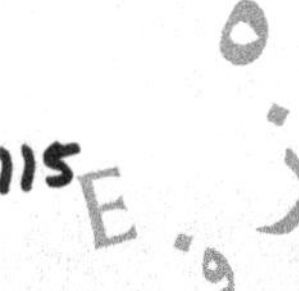

But just as scary, heart-stopping, terrible things happen in this life, miracles also happen.

The miracle was that on that particular day, 4 June, I had been sent home from school at 9.45 am – with a stomach bug. Samir was already at home, because he'd got the bug first and had been throwing up all night. I'd started feeling queasy at school that morning, and my teacher, Mrs Zamani, sent me home to recover. The guards stormed the school, looking for me, just a few hours after that. Thankfully I wasn't there. After they gave up and left, Mrs Zamani called my parents in a panic. She told them everything.

That's the moment my parents decided to flee Iran. Maman said that she could handle being captured. Even losing her life. But not mine or Samir's. She wasn't going to let them anywhere near us. It was time to leave.

I never went back to school after that day.

Never got to say goodbye to my classmates. To Mrs Zamani.

To Amir.

Aria → Amir

I want to devote this chapter to Amir. I miss him every day. And I'm sure he misses me. He was the best 'best friend' anyone could ask for.

We met on the first day of kindergarten when I saw him flying across the playground. He was sitting on one end of a seesaw, casually eating his lunch, when a Year 6 boy, Reza Mahmoodi (an Iranian Rufus equivalent) approached him, laughed and said, 'Have a nice flight, kid!'

He then came crashing down on the other end of the seesaw. Amir, who was less than half Reza's size, went FLYING. I was eating my lunch, Maman's delicious *fesenjoon*, when I saw Amir take flight . . . it was like a superhero movie.

Is it a bird?
A plane?
No, it's . . . Super Amir!

Amir seemed to fly through the air in slow motion. I couldn't believe it. Reza and his friends laughed hysterically. Amir soon came crashing down. *THUD!* He hit his head on the monkey bars and blood came gushing out. Reza and his friends quickly scattered.

I rushed over to help Amir. I wrapped my school tie around his head to stop the bleeding then ran to tell the teachers. Amir was rushed to hospital that day and ended up with six stitches on his forehead. He had a scar after that, which earnt him the nickname Harry (Potter, obviously) from then on. Reza was never punished. But he never came near Amir again.

Amir and I were inseparable after that day. He always said that he was glad Reza had sent him flying. He believed that everything happens for a reason. Reza's cruel and stupid act had triggered the kindness of many others, including me. We may never have become friends otherwise. He was also grateful for his scar. He truly loved it. Said it was a permanent reminder of the day our friendship was born. Plus, it made him look a little bit tough. Amir was philosophical like that. I always thought his nickname should've been Dumbledore instead of Harry. But he wasn't wise and serious all of the time. He could also be very cheeky. A real prankster. He loved playing tricks on people.

One year, on his birthday, he baked garlic cookies and handed them out to the whole class. He laughed so hard as everyone tried to politely swallow the disgusting biscuit.

Sometimes he'd rope me into his trickery. We'd tie people's shoelaces to their chairs in the library. One of us would distract the victim, the other would tie. And one time, he left a fake plastic dog poo on the substitute teacher's desk. Thankfully, she found it funny. So did the whole class.

None of Amir's tricks were mean-spirited. He would always own up to them, laughing and apologising at the same time. And his laugh was infectious. When he laughed, all those around him would too. It wasn't a choice. It was impossible to keep a straight face when he had the giggles.

Amir and I were like brothers. He always had my back. And I had his.

ANNOUNCEMENT ON THE SCHOOL SPEAKER

We'd only ever had two announcements over the loud speaker since I started high school. One was a fire drill. The second was this:

'Can Rufus Sherman please come to the principal's office immediately. I repeat, Rufus Sherman to the principal's office – NOW!'

I was in Ms Rubble's class at the time. Whispers started straight away. What was going on? A school-wide announcement was definitely serious stuff. Ms Rubble didn't appreciate the disruption. Her eyebrows formed a big black eagle again.

Ms Rubble

I'm sure you'd all like to spend the next 40 minutes speculating about that announcement, but I encourage you to pipe down.

Us

(Whispering)

Ms Rubble

Zip it.

Us

(More whispering)

Ms Rubble

SHUSH!!

As scary as Ms Rubble is when she's angry, her fury didn't stop the chatter. This was a historic moment. The school's biggest bully seemed to be in trouble and we all wanted confirmation. Phones started buzzing. Even though they were on 'silent', you could still hear the vibrating *buzz, buzz, buzz* of messages coming through.

Ms Rubble went around the class and confiscated every phone she could find. But not before the news was out. I finally discovered what was going on from my usual source – Jaz.

She told me that Olivia Quilty told . . .

Kamala Zein . . .

who told Leo Evans . . .

who told *her* that somebody had dobbed Doofus in for hurting Aria.

Finally! Someone (I still think it was Jaz – don't you?) had exposed Doofus. Things escalated fast after that. Doofus disappeared from the campus. We looked for him at recess but he was nowhere to be found. There were endless rumours about what had happened to him. Which do you think are true?

* Mr Hardball, our ferocious principal, had made Doofus eat 400 doughnuts and then run laps around the oval until he puked his guts up and had to be carried away on a stretcher.
* Police had arrested Doofus for rolling Ms Fit (our PE teacher) for her Nike TNs.
* The Doof had been abducted by a group of senior citizens on his way to the principal's office and forced to be the MC at their bingo nights.

Okay, so the details of what happened to him were sketchy at best but one thing that was certain was that he was suspended. Of course, it wasn't hard to guess why. He'd pinned Aria to the ground out in the open, where anyone could've seen it. Then there were all the other times he'd hurt Aria. It was hard to know which particular Doofy crime had landed him in hot water. But it didn't matter. The only thing that mattered was that he was gone. For now.

Finally, we could all breathe.

Aria → the wedding

Breathe in.

And . . . out.

Maman's breathing was deliberately measured after she got off the phone from Mrs Zamani. She pulled me and Samir into a calm embrace. I could see the panic in her eyes. And in my father's. But they were both acting serene, as if nothing out of the ordinary was happening. Their peaceful resolve unsettled me. I could sense something wasn't right. Why weren't they panicking? So many thoughts raced through my head. I looked at Samir. He was pale. Probably from the stomach bug, but maybe not. Maybe he, too, was feeling the enormity of what was about to happen. Maybe the blood was draining from his cheeks because he knew that our lives were about to change forever.

'Do we have to leave Iran?' I asked Maman, hoping against hope that she'd say no. But she didn't say no.

She didn't say anything. She just looked at me with sad eyes and stroked my hair. I burst into tears. I told her that I didn't want to leave. All that I knew and loved was here. She kissed my forehead and told me that we wouldn't leave straight away. We would go on a lovely holiday first and think things through. Samir and I were baffled. A holiday? This was hardly the time to be lounging in the sun and sipping fancy drinks by the Caspian Sea.

Maman took another deep breath and told us that we had been invited to a family wedding in the countryside. We should start packing now because we were leaving immediately. I asked whose wedding it was. And why weren't we told about it until now? Baba said it was his cousin's wedding. Cousin Cyrus. They were going to tell us but they hadn't been sure if, with all that was going on, we'd be going. But now that the guards were closing in on us, it made sense to leave Shiraz, to buy ourselves time to figure things out.

I had never heard of Cousin Cyrus. Baba said that was because he didn't live in Shiraz. He was very dear to the family and lived in a village a few hours' drive north. I was relieved that we weren't leaving Iran immediately. Going to a random cousin's wedding – as weird as that was – was better than fleeing Iran straight away. Besides, weddings were fun! It didn't matter that Samir and I didn't know Cousin Cyrus or his wife-to-be. Or anyone at the ceremony, for that matter. We would have a good time regardless.

Persian weddings are like festivals. Joyful beyond measure. Enough food to feed an entire village for a week. Jewelled rice, kebabs, and don't even get me started on the desserts – we double-dip everything in sugary rosewater syrup. Then there's the music . . . oh, the music. Upbeat. Uplifting. Uptown funk with a lot of hip wiggles and shoulder shimmies. Every part of the body jiggles when you're dancing to Persian music. And we don't stop till the sun comes up. I couldn't wait. In that moment, I went from pure panic to excitement. I stopped thinking about the Revolutionary Guards. About what could've happened if I'd stayed at school that morning. My focus shifted entirely to the upcoming festivities. We were going to a wedding!

Samir and I were secretly hoping that during this wedding adventure, our parents would change their

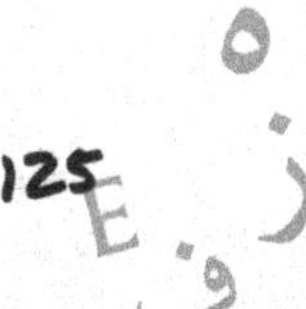

minds about leaving Iran. Perhaps they'd love the countryside so much that we'd move there. I wouldn't mind that. I mean, Shiraz was my home, but I could adjust to a village lifestyle. That would be better than leaving our homeland altogether.

Aria → dancing with Maman

Samir and I started packing for the wedding. I wanted to bring the suit I had worn to my aunt's wedding the previous year but it was still in our apartment, and we couldn't go back there in case the guards were watching the place. Then Baba told me that we wouldn't need suits. This was a village wedding so we would have to dress accordingly, in a way that respected their tribal customs. That meant Samir, Dad and I would wear long collarless shirts with brightly coloured studded vests over the top. Baggy pants and a big belt. Mum's outfit was spectacular: a floor-sweeping multi-layered skirt with colourful embroidery and sequins sewn on. I don't know where or when my parents got these outfits, but they were beautiful.

Maman danced around the room in her sparkly outfit. When she twirled, her skirt ballooned out like a spinning top.

All the sequins jingled. She could make music with her clothes. It was magical. Baba smiled and played a drumbeat on the back of the suitcase as she danced. Maman was so joyful. She lifted me up off the ground and spun me around . . .

'Dance with me, Aria *joon*.'

We danced.

We laughed.

Samir and I totally forgot about the clear and present danger we were in.

It's incredible how when the human mind shifts its focus, it can totally shift its reality. In that moment, my reality was no longer about the attempted kidnapping and another narrow escape from being captured. All I could think about was my next dance move at Cousin Cyrus's wedding. I don't want to show off but I'm a very good dancer. Maman said that I was going to steal the show away from the bride and groom with my smooth moves. And she was right. I am unbeatable on the dance floor.

Aria → Abdullah

Maman had a weak heart. She had a pacemaker which helped her regulate it. She also believed in spiritual healing methods which is why she meditated a lot. Seeing Maman in the lotus position was a familiar sight.

She was in a particularly meditative, Zen mood as we approached Abdullah – the driver who was going to take us to Cousin Cyrus's wedding. Having a driver wasn't a luxury we were used to but Baba said that since this was a special occasion, we were sparing no expense. We were going to travel there in style!

But when I saw our vehicle, I questioned my dad's definition of 'style'. Abdullah was taking us to the wedding not in a limousine or a Bentley but in a TRUCK! Well, it was actually a cross between a truck and a ute, and it was about as old and rusty as you can imagine. Abdullah himself looked like he hadn't showered in decades, but I wasn't judging. I hate showers too. His children were also there. About a dozen of them. And his wife. Or sister? Who were all these people? Were they coming to the wedding too?

Baba told me not to ask too many questions. Another two trucks pulled up and we all packed in. We headed off to the countryside in a convoy. I was in the back seat, jammed next to Maman, Samir and two other kids. Baba sat in the front, next to Abdullah. The drive was bumpy and long. I was feeling squashed and uncomfortable. Maman wrapped her arms around me and started telling Samir and me a story. She was so good at telling stories. Her voice was sweet and mesmerising. Sometimes she told us true stories of brave and heroic people like Joan of Arc, Rosa Parks and Anne Frank. And other times silly made-up stories about man-eating frogs and cities made entirely of pizza.

That day, on that bumpy ride to the countryside, she told us a true story – of a woman called Tahirih, a 19th-century Persian poet who risked her life for the emancipation of women. Even though it was a captivating story, I found myself dozing off. Every now and then, I'd jolt awake and tune in to her voice, but sleep was calling me. Despite the rocky terrain, this journey in the back of a truck was strangely soothing. It wasn't long before I fell asleep on Maman's lap.

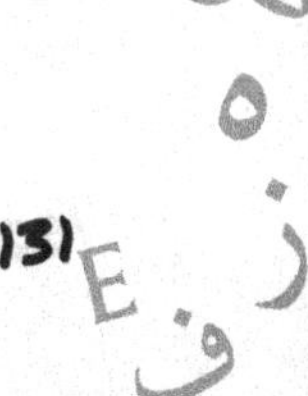

ONE GIANT LEAP

I had literally heard Aria speak once. Five words, to be precise. How was he going to go from that to performing slam poetry in front of a room full of people?

It was a big leap.

Bigger than big.

Huge.

COLOSSAL, in fact.

Imagine a toddler, taking their very first step. Wobble . . . wobble . . . fall . . . then . . . STEP! Sure, that's momentous, exciting. A cause for celebration. But it'd be absurd to think they could go from that first step to running a marathon straight away, right?

I was nervous for Aria. I didn't want to be a killjoy, but how exactly was this going to work? I decided to bring in a consultant. Luckily, I knew just the person. She was well acquainted with the client (Aria) and best of all, she was affordable. In fact, she worked for food. Doritos specifically. She demanded them as upfront payment before even agreeing to meet.

I slid the payment (my unopened packet of Cheese Supreme Doritos) across the table. It was all I had for recess, but if you want the best advice, you gotta be prepared to spend big. My consultant ripped open the packet and started scoffing them down like she was Joey Chestnut, the world's number-one competitive eater. She didn't come up for air. Didn't even offer me a single chip.

Jaz: Talk to me, babe. What can I do for ya?

Me: We need a plan, Jaz. A plan for Aria.

Jaz: Sure, sure. I hear you. A plan . . . (she paused to stuff another Dorito into her mouth) That's good. I like your thinking . . . (munch munch) Excellent idea. Big-brain stuff . . . (munch munch) A plan.

She polished off the entire packet of Doritos in record time then tilted her head back and emptied the remaining crumbs into her mouth.

Me: You good there?

She nodded thoughtfully. Looked like she was

mentally devising a plan. A brilliant plan. I was on the edge of my seat. What gem of an idea was she going to come up with? After a whole lot of staring into the distance like a philosopher, she said . . .

Jaz: What kind of plan did you have in mind exactly?

Me: JAZ!

Jaz: What?

Me: I don't have a plan! That's what I'm paying YOU for.

Jaz: To be fair, the pay was poor. It was just a mini packet.

She licked her fingers.

Jaz: But don't worry. Luckily for you – and Aria – I've got it all figured out. He is going to be fine. He's gonna ace this poetry slam thingy. Slam dunk the slam. It's gonna be beautiful.

She went on to outline her 'plan' – which, to be honest, was actually quite good. On the surface, Jaz gives the impression that she's all talk and little content . . . a whole lot of hoo-ha, smoke and mirrors. But underneath, the cogs are always turning, and she's always surprisingly brilliant. This time was no exception. She came up with a solid plan.

We were going to help Aria prepare for the comp

by forming a band. He'd be the frontman, of course. But she and I would be on stage with him. Backing him up. Giving him the moral support he needed to conquer this challenge. Kind of like a cheer squad. With instruments. I reminded Jaz that I played the piano but she didn't think that was very useful. I needed a portable instrument. She decided a tambourine would be the go. I shrugged and accepted. How hard could it be? Besides, people always look cool shaking tambourines on stage.

She declared herself the beatboxer-in-chief. I wasn't sure what that meant.

'Let me give you a demo,' she said, and then proceeded to make the most incredible sounds with her mouth. Bongo drum, snare drum, bass drum, maracas, gong . . . you name it. Did she have a whole percussion band living at the base of her tongue?

'Dude, that sounds amazing. How did you learn to do that?' I asked.

'Partly genetics, partly YouTube,' she replied.

Another part of Jaz's grand plan was that we'd help Aria get used to performing by doing gigs. Of course, we had no idea what we were doing and weren't a real band so no one was going to pay us . . . BUT, we could busk. Busking would be good practice, plus we could make a few bucks along the way. Jaz was excited by that prospect too.

'Ka-ching! We'll clean up, Hero. Grown-ups love kid performers. Especially street performers. You wait, we're gonna be big – and RICH!'

She had slipped into the 'band manager' mode with such ease. Like it was her calling. She was born to do this.

'We'll call ourselves Groucho's Humans,' she said.

'I'm sorry, whaaaat?' I responded. 'You want to name us after your slimy pet snake?'

'Yes!' she said. 'I can beatbox with him wrapped around my shoulders. Also, snakes aren't slimy. That's a myth.'

'No, Jaz. Slimy or not, just . . . no.'

'Trust me, Groucho will give us the street cred we need. People respect snakes.'

'People are terrified of snakes! Besides, we'll look like some kind of freak show if you're beatboxing with a big yellow python wrapped around your neck!'

We agreed to disagree on Groucho's involvement, for now. I reminded her that this was not about her or her unconventional animal companions. It was about

Aria. Jaz sighed but admitted that she had got slightly carried away and that it was best not to let personal ambition overtake this mission.

So how exactly was our band going to help Aria skyrocket his way to fame . . . and Edinburgh? Good question. We weren't entirely sure, but we knew that having us and the band would surely make him feel more at ease. We were going to help him master his vocal skills. Get that voice of his to come out again . . . out from its currently bolted-up box.

This wasn't going to be easy. But at least we had a plan. Jaz had come good. She had delivered. I was happy. Money (in form of Doritos) well spent. Now we had to present our plan to the heavyweight poetry champion himself, and see what he thought.

Aria → border control

I woke up to the sound of guards shouting. We seemed to be at some kind of checkpoint. I sat up and looked out the window. The landscape was barren. Harsh. Unforgiving. Dirt roads and tree-less mountains as far as the eye could see. There were a few demountable buildings which looked more like tin sheds patched together by mud. Dozens of uniformed guards swarmed the place like flies. A couple of them were having an exchange with Abdullah through the truck window. It didn't look friendly. One of them banged on the side of the truck and shouted at Abdullah to hurry up.

'Yalla, zood bash!'

He was asking for our paperwork. Paperwork? I couldn't work out what was going on. This particularly angry guard had a gun. A big gun slung over his shoulder. Maybe this village had extra security, I thought.

I called out from the back seat. '*Agha*, why do we need paperwork to go to a wedding?'

Baba's head swung around so fast I thought he'd give himself whiplash.

He gave me a look.

A 'shut up' look.

I was confused.

Maman tightened her grip around me and Samir. She pulled us closer, into an embrace that almost hurt.

The guard stuck his leathery face through the driver's window and looked at us all crammed in the back. I thought we might get a fine for having too many people squashed together with no seatbelts. But I was starting to realise that that wasn't the issue. If this was a routine stop, Baba's nails wouldn't be digging into the torn, vinyl seat covers. His knuckles wouldn't be white. His face even more white.

Abdullah shoved some papers into the guard's hands. He looked at them. Flipped a few pages. Then went back a page. He screwed up his face. He poked his head into the car once more and looked at us again. Me, Maman and Samir. As well as Abdullah's two children.

His stare was intense.

His silence, deafening.

My heart started pounding.

I didn't like this.

I didn't like it at all.

I wasn't sure what was happening, but it wasn't good. Maman's grip on me tightened. Samir's head lowered. Abdullah's children grabbed each other's hands.

The guard told Abdullah to wait. He then took the papers and walked over to some other guards. The men began talking to each other. Pointing at the papers and discussing something.

I could sense the panic rising in my throat.

I started to feel short of breath.

Just couldn't seem to fill my lungs with enough air.

There wasn't enough air!

I needed answers.

What was going on?

Why were we here?

Who were those men?

But I knew I couldn't ask anything right now. It was not the time. Baba's look had told me that, only moments prior. I looked up at Maman – beads of sweat were trickling down her face. Genuine fear in her eyes.

I had never seen her look so scared. I knew just by looking at her that we weren't going to a wedding.

In that moment I knew we were trying to escape Iran.

While the guards debated over our papers, Abdullah exchanged a look with Baba.

Baba nodded.

Abdullah put his foot to the pedal.

Too much acceleration caused the wheels of the truck to spin and make a screeching noise.

We must have gone from zero to a hundred in mere seconds.

The guards frantically ran after our truck. The friction of our tyres against the surface of the dirt road created a huge dust cloud. For a few moments, we couldn't see the guards. Or the border control station, for that matter.

Abdullah was banging on the steering wheel, begging his tired old truck to go faster. Faster than it had ever gone before.

'Come on! *Joon bekan!*'

As the dust settled, I saw a few of the guards in the distance, hunched over and puffed out from running.

Abdullah looked in his rear-view mirror and

shouted something unintelligible. Then he laughed. A triumphant laugh.

I was both terrified and relieved.

We were on our way to freedom.

Band practice

Aria was ALL IN. His eyes lit up when we pitched him our band idea. We decided that we would have to practise somewhere other than school, mainly because Aria couldn't access his voice at school. I offered my place. The garage, to be specific. Teen movies always have bands practising their music in someone's garage. I felt cooler just thinking about it.

Aria. This was about Aria. I had to keep reminding myself of that! Not about me and the fact that I was about to go from boring, reliable Hero to . . .

Hero the uber-cool, tambourine goddess.

Aria laughed. He didn't agree that this was all about him. The way he saw it, this band was a celebration of our friendship. Our quirky little gang. He said (or rather, he *wrote*) that he knew deep in his heart that the three of us would be friends for life. Jaz punched him in the arm and told him not to be so sappy.

He smiled.

So did I.

None of us wanted to admit that we were feeling sentimental about the birth of this band, but we all knew we were starting something special. It was going to be awesome.

My dad had prepped the garage for our very first band practice. He had set up a mic and speakers, laid out an overly fluffy brown carpet that looked like Mr Snuffleupagus roadkill and stocked the bar fridge with good eats and fizzy drinks. There were veggie wraps (for Jaz, who was vegan this week), meatball subs (for me and Aria, shameless carnivores), not to mention ice-cream, jelly and even pumpkin pie (my favourite) which Dad made from scratch. My dad can be so extra.

He also nominated himself 'director of operations'. None of us knew what that meant exactly. Sounded like some kind of boss in a spy movie. My dad, the James Bond of poetry. Insert laughing emoji here.

Dad said that we could laugh but that slam poetry was serious business. It required training. Hardcore training. It was the contact sport of words. You couldn't just show up and nail it, even if you *did* have a voice. In Aria's case, it was going to be particularly difficult. He needed a coach to help him with all the various hurdles.

Dad was just the person for the job. He was able to use the techniques he'd learnt over the years to deal with his own battles. He knew better than anybody that it's possible for the body to freeze up when emotions are running the show. The mind will always find ways to cope. But sometimes that coping looks like not coping. It looks like sadness. Or muteness. Or stage fright. It was great that Dad was still in an UP cycle, because it meant that he could help Aria by doing what he does best – teach.

Professor Rodriguez, aka Dad, is known for being the best, most entertaining lecturer at his uni. When he's not feeling DOWN, not sinking into the quicksand of his emotions (as he puts it), he's larger than life. Confident. Funny. Exuberant. His spirit fills every room. And his students love him. They call him 'O Captain! My Captain!' – a reference to some old Robin Williams movie.

Before our first rehearsal, Dad treated us to one of his motivational pep talks. He taught Aria to use a method called **A-B-C-D-E** to help him access his voice and overcome his anxiety in front of a crowd.

- → **A – ACCEPT** everything just as it is.
- → **B – BREATHE** in . . . out . . . it's so easy, but sometimes we all forget to do it.
- → **C – CENTRE** and focus on your core strength. That mega-flex feeling that comes from the pit of your belly.
- → **D – DECIDE** on your path. What you're going to do.
- → **E – ENGAGE** with the world. With your audience. With life. Show 'em who's boss!

Jaz was loving this. Eating it up. I mean, she's hardly in need of a confidence boost. If anything, she has a surplus of confidence. An oversupply. That girl has self-love pouring out of every fibre of her being. Not in an arrogant way; no, Jaz isn't up herself. She just knows she's awesome and she's not afraid to own it. Some people spend their whole lives trying to develop that kind of self-assurance but for Jaz, it comes easily. She was born ready.

Aria hadn't said a word – yet – but I could tell by the beaming smile on his face that he was appreciating Dad too. Here was someone who understood him. And believed in him. Believed that he could smash out a poetry jam in front of a room full of people and kill it . . . even though he could barely speak.

Aria → the chase

I could barely speak as Abdullah stepped on the accelerator and sped off . . . away from my life as I knew it.

I managed to mumble out a few words.

'We're not going to a wedding, are we, Baba?'

'No, we're leaving Iran, Aria *joon*.'

Samir chimed in with questions of his own.

Why hadn't they told us?

Why pretend we were going to a wedding?

We both felt confused and betrayed. Baba tried to explain that it was for our own safety. It wouldn't have been wise to let us know, in case we got stopped and interrogated. We realised that we were dressed this way so that we'd blend in with Abdullah's Kurdish family for the escape. Not for Cousin Cyrus's wedding. In fact, there was no Cousin Cyrus. And Abdullah wasn't our driver. My parents had paid him to smuggle us out of the country.

All this information came in dribs and drabs as we navigated the rocky terrain at 150 kilometres per hour in an old beaten-up truck.

I was being thrown around that back seat with every turn. My head hit the roof of the truck. It hurt but I didn't feel any pain. Adrenaline masks pain.

Maman and Baba kept looking behind us – making sure that the guards weren't pursuing us. To check we were, in fact, safe from harm.

And that's when I heard the sound . . .

The piercing sound of sirens.

My mother tightened her grip around me. I looked up at her. Her dark skin had turned pale. Almost white.

The siren was getting louder and louder.

That could only mean one thing.

The Revolutionary Guards were on our trail . . . and they were drawing closer to us.

I thought that there must be nothing more frightening than the sound of a siren getting closer.

I was wrong.

BANG!

Gunshots started firing.

BANG!
BANG!
BANG!

I wanted to scream but I couldn't.

Nobody could.

There were no panicked cries of fear or dread. Of sheer terror.

Terror has no sound.

It is deadly silent.

Time stood still.

While also hurtling ahead at lightning speed, tripping over itself.

Maman pushed our heads down into our laps.

'Stay down,' she said, her voice trembling. 'Stay down!'

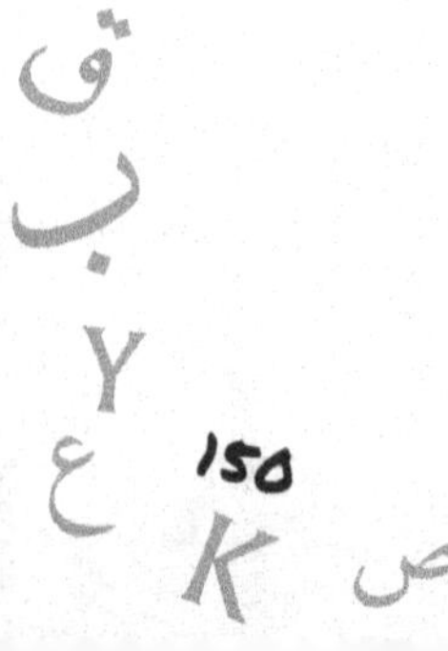

BUSKING IN THE SUN

Aria wasn't mute during band practice but he wasn't exactly Sir Talk-a-lot either. Dad suggested small steps. Aria didn't have to launch into reciting full poems from the get-go. Jaz and I could fill in for him until he felt comfortable. Aria liked this idea. So did Jaz. Me? No way. I can jiggle a tambourine, do back-up vocals, even bust out the occasional dance move, but I wasn't about to dive into slam poetry.

Aria also requested that we didn't use his award-winning poem until the day of the competition. Jaz and I didn't really understand why. Dad thought that maybe the poem was too personal, too triggering for Aria to have to recite over and over again. Truth is, we didn't really know. None of us had even read his poem yet. He teased us and said we'd have to wait till the comp. We were going to hear it along with everyone else on the day.

So we rehearsed using other poems. We chose a few together. Poems by Rumi (Aria's favourite poet), Tupac (Jaz's fave) and, since I didn't really have a favourite poet, I chose one of Dad's all-time favourite poems: 'No Man is an Island'.

We rehearsed and rehearsed . . . and then rehearsed some more. After school, on the weekends, any chance we got. We were having so much fun. It was a welcome distraction from school, even though school was no longer stressful because Doofus had been suspended for three weeks.

The first time we jammed, we sounded awful. I'm not being modest. We were bad. Really bad. Jaz's previously dope beatboxing skills suddenly sounded offbeat and tinny. My tambourine game was NOT on point. It takes skill to stuff up the tambourine and yet, somehow, I was managing to make us sound like the Wiggles instead of Bob Dylan. Not cool.

And Aria? True to form, he didn't say a word. We were expecting him to chime in, but no such luck. He watched Jaz and I fumble our way through the first 'slam' and when it was over, he just looked at us . . . with a kind of shocked face. Then, after a few uncomfortable moments, he spoke . . .

'That was . . . bad.'

Jaz lost it. She laughed so hard that tears started to flow and she had to bend over to recover. Then I got the giggles. It was true, we stank. And for some reason, we didn't find this alarming. It was just funny. Jaz fell to the floor, clutching her belly, barely able to speak, but she managed to choke out: 'You're right, man. We suck!'

Aria did a facepalm and started laughing too. Laughing in a time of crisis is a kind of madness. We had clearly lost the plot, so we decided to call it quits and try again another day.

Amazingly, we got better.

We persevered through some patchy times, but with each practice, we improved a bit more. We went from sounding like a totally disastrous car crash of a band to . . .

half okay to . . .

pretty good.

With each session we grew more comfortable with our style and sense of rhythm. Some days Aria struggled to say a single word, other days he could recite entire lines of poetry. Hearing him speak was magical. I will never tire of hearing his voice. It appears like a gift when you least expect it.

Finally, after three weeks of solid jamming sessions, we were ready to perform. So, we psyched ourselves up and we did it.

We busked!

On the street.

In the sun.

In all our wondrous glory.

We ended up calling ourselves The Snake Charmers. Jaz's idea of having Groucho join the band was a hit with Dad and Aria so I was out-voted on that one. And Jaz was right, Groucho was a big drawcard. Aria was surprisingly comfortable handling him. In fact, Aria was the one who held him during our act, not Jaz. He draped the reptile around his shoulders like some sort of slinky, slithery shawl and kind of danced around with him as he made his way to and from the mic.

Jaz would gracefully move between beatboxing and reciting poems. I dominated on the tambourine. And Aria would chime in with a significant word or sentence from time to time.

Each time he uttered a word in public was a triumph.

And if you didn't know he was sometimes mute, you'd think that this was just our jam. Part of our act. Our particular style of performance poetry where the dude with the snake was like some kind of goth–emo guest vocalist. Which couldn't be further from the truth. Aria is neither goth nor emo. He's usually quite sunny. But if you wear black, hang a snake around your neck and speak sparingly, then 'goth' is definitely the vibe you're giving off.

Our musical poetry was unique. Bit jammy. Bit soul. Bit punk rock. You couldn't really define it, but I have to say that for three people who hadn't really performed anything before, we were pretty good. And we drew a decent crowd. Not enough to fill the Opera House, but enough.

We set up just outside the local supermarket so there was good foot traffic. Our audience was a mixed bag which included Joseph, the local (and vocal) homeless man who would cheer and holler as we performed, as well as little kids who would lunge towards Groucho just to see if he was a real snake. Nervous parents would politely pull their children back and watch from a safe distance. We also had the high schoolers. They loved to loiter and watch us perform.

We felt pretty gangster when a group of Year 10 or 11 kids would stop by and groove along to our sound. And everyone who stopped and listened would throw us a few coins.

My dad watched from a distance. He beamed as he directed people towards our little trio in his enthusiastic, UP kind of way. I wasn't sure what I was happier about – the fact that we were helping Aria in his poetry pursuit (and having so much fun in the process) or seeing Dad light up while he watched our performance.

Our repertoire consisted of only three poems, or beats, as Jaz called them, so we performed them in a loop, with breaks in between. We did three loops of three songs and made $41.60.

Jaz took her $13.85 and blew it all immediately. Bought herself Fanta, Sour Patches and the Big Kahuna Burger from the new burger joint around the corner from her house.

Aria → 'My heart'

BANG!
BANG!

The gunshots continued. Abdullah made a sudden jerky turn and veered off the highway into the desert. It was the only way he could lose the guards. His truck, as rusty and old as it was, was made for off-road. I noticed that Maman was beginning to gasp for air. She was clutching her heart. Her weak heart.

'It's okay, Aria *joon*. Everything is going to be okay,' she said to me, trying to sound reassuring, but I was worried.

The wheels got bogged in the sand. The desert terrain was too soft. Baba jumped out and began pushing the truck. The guards had followed us but they got stuck too. It became a race against time. We had to beat them. There was no other option. I looked at

Maman. She was looking up, pleading with the heavens. Still clutching her chest.

The wheels were spinning but we weren't moving forward. Sand was flicking into the air like a fountain, covering Baba as he pushed and pushed. His hair was dripping with sweat. His face contorted, straining. Abdullah was revving the truck and frustratedly banging his hand on the steering wheel.

'*Boro digeh!*' he shouted at his rusty old friend. 'Go, go, go!'

Time, being the strange and mysterious illusion that it is, once again stood still. I felt both desperate and detached. Like I was watching this terrifying scene from above.

Then, with a mighty push from Baba, the wheels finally came unstuck and the truck jerked into motion. Baba ran and leapt into the passenger seat as we accelerated forward. He was panting, trying to catch his breath. I looked behind us. The guards were still struggling to free their car. They fired a few more shots, but we were getting further and further away from them. It was a relief to see their car get smaller and smaller as we drove off.

We kept driving for what seemed like an eternity.

Perhaps it was only a few kilometres, perhaps a few hundred. I don't know. But eventually we lost them.

I should have been happy in that moment.

We had made it.

We had escaped an oppressive regime that was choking our freedom. Our rights. Our very lives.

But I didn't feel free.

I felt suffocated as I looked up at Maman.

She was struggling to breathe.

I felt her every gasp as if it were mine.

Baba took one look at her and panicked.

He jumped into the back seat while the car was moving, frantically swapping places with Abdullah's children.

'Mona!' he shouted as he desperately held on to her. 'Tell me you're okay, *azizam*. Please!'

But Maman wasn't okay.

She said just two words . . .

'My heart.'

The fear of the gunshots, the fear of being caught, the fear of losing us . . . all of it had impacted her weak heart.

She was not okay.

But she was calm.

She knew she wasn't going to make it but she told us to be strong. And brave.

Samir began to cry. Uncontrollable tears. He started cursing the guards, the regime, the government. He was angry. Really angry.

'I hate them!' he said. 'I hate those fundamentalist tyrants!'

Maman pulled him towards her chest. She closed her eyes and she smiled. As though she had one foot in the next world already. There was something remarkably peaceful about her in that moment. She spoke softly to Samir. Told him that he must never let hate into his heart. 'It will ruin you,' she said.

She reached over and pulled me close to her too. I felt her warm breath on my forehead as I pressed my cheek into her chest. 'My boys . . . my beautiful boys. Look after each other. And your baba.'

She wrapped her arms around us like a cocoon.

'Stay true to your beliefs,' she said. 'Always fight for justice . . . but do it with love. No matter how difficult it gets.'

I listened as she spoke about the power of love.

Revolutionary love.

Radical love.

'A love so big, that it can swallow "hate" whole and burp out a rainbow.'

Baba held his wife in his arms. By now, he, too, seemed calm. Accepting. He knew just how fragile her heart condition was and seeing her in that weakened state, it was obvious to him that she wouldn't last the journey.

I was filled with grief.

And fear.

I didn't understand. How could she speak of love when she was being pursued to her death by hateful, angry people?

I rejected a love that big. A love that forgiving. That kind of love was not for me.

RETURN OF THE DOOFUS

The three weeks without Doofus were bliss. We roamed around the school like we owned it. Not always looking over our shoulder, waiting for the big oaf to strike again. And even though Aria was still not talking at school, he was a lot happier. His whole demeanour had changed from 'mysterious chill guy' to 'happy, upbeat guy'. He had a spring in his step. And he even pranked us once, in his uniquely wordless way. Brought a batch of homemade cookies to school and shared them with us. Jaz and I hoed right in, expecting another delicious Persian treat. Instead we took one bite and nearly puked. They tasted like butt. I'm not even kidding. You've never tasted anything so putrid in your life.

Aria watched us chew, swallow some and spit the remaining bits out.

'Duuuuuude! What is this festy biscuit made of?' asked Jaz, still spitting and spluttering. Aria burst out laughing. He laughed so hard, he couldn't respond. Jaz and I ran for the bubblers, trying to get the gross taste out of our mouths. The more we squealed and complained, the more he cacked himself. He finally wrote down what was in the cookies . . .

Three jars of crushed garlic!

He wiped tears from his eyes as he confessed to pranking us with a trick he'd learnt from a friend back in Iran. Jaz declared war. She was furious – in a not-really-serious kind of way. She chased him around the yard, seeking revenge in the form of a dead arm. He was going to cop it big time.

And that's when all the fun and games came to a sudden halt. Aria, who was laughing and dodging Jaz with some sweet sidestepping techniques, ran straight into . . .

DOOFUS!

Gulp. He was back.

Everybody froze. Including Doofus, which was weird. Somehow, time froze as well.

I closed my eyes and prayed for a miracle. Life had been so good with Doofus away. I didn't want things to return to how they were. Couldn't Aria be magically teleported in that moment? Away from Doofus's glare. Like when Harry Potter disappeared from the 'now' and went back in time with Hermione's time-turner?

We waited with bated breath. Surely Doofus wasn't going to go back to his old thuggish ways after a three-week suspension? Even *he* wasn't that stupid.

Doofus took a menacing step towards Aria. Jaz looked at me in dismay, and her face said, *here we go again*. Aria studied the floor. Finally, Doofus spoke . . .

'Okay, Mute Boy. You win. I'm waving me white flag. Can ya see it?' Doofus waved his hand holding an invisible flag in the air. Aria took a step back, confused. Doofus continued. 'Game. Set. Match. To the little squirt with no voice. I gotta hand it to ya, Mutey, you got me good. The diary posts, the snitching . . . some shady tricks, bruh. Respect.'

Aria's eyes widened. He looked at me and Jaz. We shrugged, just as shocked.

'So, what do you say we call a truce? I'll lay off ya and you stop posting pages of me diary. Deal?'

In that historic moment, something unbelievable happened. Can you guess which of the following?

1: Aria did a Karate Kid swivel and kick, and knocked Doofus to the ground.

2: Aria agreed to the truce, reached into his bag and handed Doofus back the infamous little yellow diary.

3: Aria literally started doing the moonwalk dance move away from Doofus, which made everybody laugh. It was a good distraction because it threw The Doof, and Aria ran for the hills.

Okay, I was teasing you. It's none of the above. Here's what actually happened.

Alfie Toogood – remember him? Yes, Alfie stepped in, like some kind of action hero at the end of a movie, and handed Doofus his diary. Then he said . . .

'Deal!'

We all gasped.

Doofus was more shocked than all of us. He looked at his friend, confused. Alfie took a deep breath and came clean.

'I was sick of seeing you push him around, bruh. He's not even half your size. Look at the kid . . . he's puny! And he doesn't speak a word,' said Alfie, trying to explain his reasoning for this great betrayal.

Doofus was stunned. His jaw literally dropped. Now *he* was lost for words.

Alfie continued. 'You were never gonna stop, bruh. And it was too brutal to watch. I had to do sumfink.'

And there was more. Turns out, it was Alfie who dobbed Doofus in to the principal. That film he took of Aria being pinned to the ground was all the evidence Mr Hardball needed to suspend Rufus.

None of us had seen this coming. Doofus's own people had turned on him! It was the ultimate betrayal. An inside job. Heads were gonna roll. Or maybe not. Maybe Doofus had finally come to the end of his reign of terror. Maybe his time was up and this was the beautiful 'poetic justice' end of it all.

A speechless Doofus looked down at his diary. The shock of it had really made him mute. He didn't shout or curse or even push Alfie. He just hugged the diary close to his chest and stared at his mate in utter disbelief. Alfie was acting far too casual, considering the gravity of this moment.

'Don't hassle the kid and there won't be any more trouble. Are we sweet?'

Doofus swallowed hard. Then nodded. They were sweet. This was it. The end of the road.

After that, the buzz about Doofus shifted. He was no longer front-page news. Kids are fickle like that.

One minute someone's hated, the next minute no one cares. The school news cycle moves fast. You can go from 'talk of the town' to irrelevant in a nanosecond. From powerful to totally cancelled in an instant.

We watched Doofus and Alfie walk away. This was one encounter we'd never forget.

Aria → forget me not

Many thoughts raced through my mind in those last moments of Maman's life. How could we go on without her? She was the captain of our ship. The heart of the family. The pulsating force. I couldn't imagine a life without my maman. But what I was most afraid of was forgetting her. I was only nine. What if my memories of her faded with time? Like sand blown away by a breeze. What if I couldn't hold on to them despite trying my hardest?

I begged Maman to stay. But sleep was calling her. Eternal sleep.

I held on to her limp hand. If I could just stop her soul from escaping her body, maybe she would live?

But she was on her way out. Her breathing became laboured. Her eyes heavy.

Baba and Samir wept quietly.

But not me.

I looked at my beautiful maman, desperate to find a way.

A way to ensure I'd never forget her.

Would I keep a lock of her hair? Put it in my pocket and never, ever lose it?

Or perhaps I'd take the gold and turquoise necklace from around her neck and wear it? Wear it until I became a wrinkly old man?

No, no . . .

That wasn't the answer.

Material things vanish. They get lost. Or break into a thousand pieces.

I needed to find a better way. A way to keep her with me forever.

And then it came to me.

Amir's scar.

The one he got from being flung across the schoolyard. He always said that he was grateful for that permanent mark on his forehead, because it reminded him of the day we met. Of our friendship. Of us.

That's what I needed too. A scar that would forever remind me of Maman.

Of her final words.

Of her bigger-than-big love.

And so, I asked her to do one last thing for me.

I asked her to bite me.

So that I could carry the scar – and her – around with me for the rest of my life.

Baba told me not to be crazy.

But I was determined.

I begged Maman.

Begged her to leave me something to remember her by.

A visible, permanent mark that no one could ever take away.

Maman's eyes filled with tears.

She took my hand. She kissed it, ever so gently. And then, as she quietly and peacefully slipped away from this world, she bit deep into my middle finger. Yes, the rude one. She bit me until my blood began to flow.

With her last breath, she gave me my final wish.

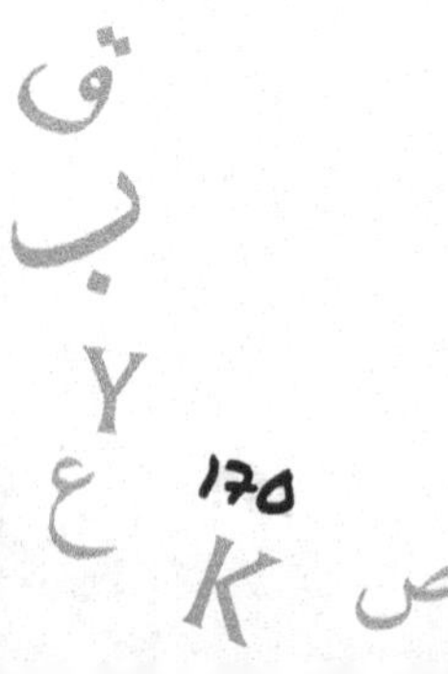

COMP NIGHT

The time had finally come. The poetry slam competition was upon us. It was being held at an old theatre, one of those retro ones with velvet curtains, stained carpet, and chandeliers. We rocked up early just to get ourselves into the zone. Aria especially needed that extra time. Even though he was now happier than I'd ever seen him before and speaking more frequently, it was still a big deal for him to stand up in front of all those people and perform. It's a big deal for anyone, let alone a mostly silent kid.

Mum drove us to the venue and did all the boring registration stuff at the door. We were so pumped. The only thing weighing on my heart was that Dad wasn't there. His UP mood had taken a bit of a downward turn. He wasn't spiralling (as Mum calls it) but he wasn't well enough for crowds either. He did manage to help us prep for the big night, though. Gave Aria one of those Muhammad Ali inspirational pep talks. Reminded him to BREATHE, and to believe in himself. Both easier said than done when you're up there in front of a big crowd. Aria seemed in control. Cool as a cucumber. But that didn't mean he was. I've learnt that people can appear one way on the outside and feel completely the opposite on the inside.

The place was buzzing when we got there. There were all sorts of people: contestants, parents, judges and poetry fans. An official-looking woman with thick black-rimmed glasses and white hair that was styled into a kind of mohawk welcomed Aria. She knew exactly who he was.

'You must be Aria,' she said enthusiastically from across the room. For a smallish-sized woman, she had a very big voice. Had she swallowed a microphone?

Aria smiled as she made a beeline for him, hand stretched out ready to shake.

'I love your work,' she said.

Jaz and I looked at her. Was she serious? She sounded like a pompous Hollywood producer schmoozing a famous actor. Without meaning to, Jaz and I giggled at her over-the-top greeting. But Aria shook her hand and grinned from ear to ear.

I think he could easily get used to the celebrity lifestyle.

She showed us around the theatre, pointing out the stage where we'd be performing as well as backstage, where we'd get ready. It was like a maze back there; so many different rooms, corridors, arrows pointing to the stage, to the toilets, to the control room. What even is that?

It was all becoming very real. My heart started to race. I was only playing the tambourine and I was nervous. I wondered how Aria was feeling. This was his gig. He was the man of the hour. Surely, he was nervous too?

Aria → comp night

I was terrified!

How did I end up here?

What was I thinking?

I had said yes to all of it because I knew that it would have made Maman proud. All along, I could hear her voice, encouraging me to use mine. To tell our story to the world.

But now that I was here, about to go up in front of all these people, I was petrified. Frozen.

Baba and Samir arrived just before the competition was about to begin. They had brought a tray of Persian sweets. It's customary in our culture to offer sweets when something good happens. Baba had been up all night making halva. The smell of rosewater and saffron was soothing but I couldn't eat anything. Baba insisted. He said it would bring me good luck. I took a piece of halva to be polite. Pretended to eat it but quietly slipped it into my pocket when he wasn't looking.

Jaz, who was stuffing the sweets into her mouth, thanked my dad and then checked her watch. It was time for us to go backstage and prepare for our performance.

Baba and Samir hugged me. Hero and Jaz's mums cheered us on and said strange things like 'chookas' and 'break a leg'. I thought that was a bit rude.

They took their seats in the audience and we headed backstage. We were ninth on the list. That gave me a bit of time to get myself together. To breathe.

But I was feeling panic rise up in my throat. All the other kids performing were English-speaking natives. They had done this before.

I was terrified.

How did I end up here?

What was I thinking?

LIGHTS, CAMERA, CHOKE!

Aria looked freaked. He went mute again. Jaz tried to shake him out of it. She even did the Daggy Dance, but it was futile. He didn't even crack a smile. He just looked through us like a zombie. I reminded him to breathe. That seemed to work for a moment. He nodded then took a deep breath.

'Atta boy!' said Jaz. 'Don't flip out. You're gonna be fine!'

But he wasn't fine. The colour drained from his face. He looked like he was going to faint. I told him to go to the bathroom and splash some water on his face.

He nodded enthusiastically and managed to say a few words. 'Yes, good idea.'

He swung open the bathroom door and marched in.

Aria → the urinal climb

I marched into the bathroom. Waited for the door to stop swinging, then when I was completely out of Jaz and Hero's sight, I looked for an escape route. Luckily there were three windows above the men's urinals.

How would I navigate this? I mean, how would I actually climb up? The urinals were well placed. If I just stepped up onto the porcelain bowl, then took another step onto the steel flush, I could probably get a good grip on the windowsill. I contemplated this manoeuvre for a moment. Was I really going to climb up that stinky pee bowl and escape through those narrow toilet windows?

Or was I going to splash some water on my face and go back out there and make my maman proud?

I stood for a moment. This was a big decision but I didn't have a lot of time to think about it.

So I did what Hero's dad had taught me. I took a few deep breaths . . .

INNNNN and OUTTTT

. . . then climbed up the urinal.

Like Spider-Man. There was no stopping me. I didn't even care that I was getting splashes of wee all over my trousers as I slipped, fell and picked myself up again.

Up I went.

Up onto the window ledge.

The adrenaline made it easy. Before I knew it, I was squeezing myself through the narrow window. Head and upper torso hanging out. Tummy and legs to follow.

Ow!

It was tight. I sucked in my belly. Really should cut down on the Persian rice!

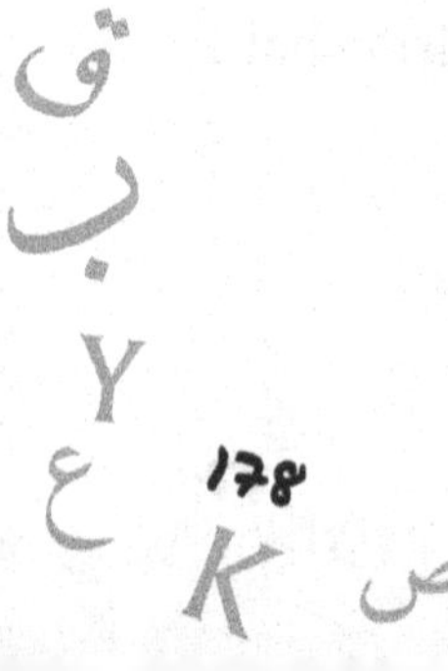

WHERE IS HE ALREADY?

We waited for ages. Waited and waited.

'How long does it take to splash a bit of water on your face?' said Jaz.

'You don't think he's hiding out in there, do you?' I asked.

Jaz said we'd give him a few more minutes and if he wasn't out, we were going in.

'But –' I didn't get to finish that sentence. She cut me off.

'NO BUTS!' She started counting. 'One missisipilly, two missisipilly . . .'

I asked her what on earth she was saying. Didn't she mean 'Mississippi'? She dismissed my query with a wave. This wasn't the time to be discussing pronunciation of American states.

We were going to be on stage in less than half an hour and our frontman was either throwing up from nerves or had a serious case of diarrhoea. Either way, he was stuck in the loo.

She didn't even get to five missisipilly before bursting into the men's toilets and shouting Aria's name. I prayed to all that was holy that there were no dudes mid-business in the lavatory, and followed her.

'ARIA!' Jaz shouted as she flung open every cubicle door. He wasn't in the first one . . . or the second . . . or the third.

Aria had vanished!

Aria → dumpster chronicles

Ouch!

I landed headfirst in a big, thorny bush. I guess that's better than concrete.

But . . . OUCH!

I got a few scrapes on my face and ripped a hole in my new T-shirt. I stood up, dusted myself off and tried to think of my next move.

Where was I going to go? I was officially on the run. This was so absurd. But I didn't have time to think about the absurdity of it all. All I knew was that I had to get away from the theatre – and from that stage – as fast as I could.

I ran and ran until I couldn't run anymore. My head was spinning. I figured I must be in the next suburb but when I stopped to catch my breath, I realised I was just around the other side of the theatre.

I felt dizzy. I asked my brain to cooperate with me. Desperately pleading with it to help me figure out what to do next. Surely Hero and Jaz would come looking for me and find me, standing here, in broad daylight. I had to find a place to hide.

I spotted a big blue dumpster close to the backstage door. They'd never find me in there. I didn't stop to think about how disgusting dumpsters are. I just knew that if I could somehow manage to get myself in there, I wouldn't have to go out on that stage in front of all those people.

And that was all that mattered right now.

Operation Find Aria

'Well, feed me garlic and call me stinky!' said Jaz. 'He's done a runner!' Jaz pointed to the half-open window above the urinals. We bolted out of the bathroom and headed for the door. We had to find Aria – and FAST!

As we hurried through the corridors, trying to find the exit, I ran into Mum, who was straightening her hair as she came out of the ladies' toilets.

'Hero!' she said. 'What are you doing?'

I told her that Aria had bolted. That we needed to find him, because we had to be on stage in just over 20 minutes. Mum said she'd help us look for him. The three of us ran through the complicated maze of corridors until we found the exit.

We burst through the double doors. The brightness of the sun stopped us in our tracks. It took a moment for our eyes to adjust.

'Where could he be?' asked Mum.

We looked around. No sign of him at all. The only things we could see were the theatre car park, packed with cars, and an adjacent suburban street where a man was walking his dog. This was a disaster. We were never going to find Aria. He'd obviously run as fast and as far as he could.

Jaz suggested that we split up and go in different directions. One of us was bound to find him, she said hopefully. I slumped. Even if we *did* run in different directions and eventually found him, it would be too late. We were on in less than 20 minutes. If we didn't find him in the next five, we'd lose our spot in the program and Aria's shot at winning this thing would have flown out the window. (Pun fully intended.)

Aria → 'Maman, can you hear me?'

I sat motionless in the dark.

Inside a giant industrial bin.

Amid the stench of the rubbish – rotten tinned spaghetti, a fishbone, used nappies. Blurrghhh.

I held my breath. It really did stink.

In the quiet solitude of that absurd moment, I got to thinking . . .

Why was I hiding? Running away from the one thing that I wanted most. To share my words with the world?

Truth was, I didn't know. I didn't want things to end this way. I had worked so hard for this. Jaz, Hero and her dad had worked hard for this, too. They'd supported me. Guided me. Given so much of their time and hearts. And this was how I was repaying them. By running away and diving headfirst into a pile of smelly trash.

And yet, I felt paralysed. The same way I did when it came to speaking at school. The will was there, but the ability simply wasn't. I didn't feel able. Able to drag myself out of the rubbish. To return to the theatre. To stand in front of dozens of strangers and perform. To share my story with the world in such an exposing way. What if they hated it? Worse still, what if they were indifferent? What if my voice didn't show up and I got booed off the stage?

There were so many 'what ifs'.

I decided to talk to Maman. Yes, I know she's not alive. But that's one of the perks of having someone in heaven. You can talk to them any time you want. It's a hard thing to explain. And you probably wouldn't believe me if I tried. But sometimes, if I can manage to block out the world around me and talk to her directly . . . she responds. Not in words, of course. In other ways. Mysterious ways.

I closed my eyes.

Squeezed them shut.

And I spoke.

Not out loud.

In my head.

She's good at hearing my inner voice.

'Maman, can you hear me? Can you see me? Over here, in the big blue bin. Yes, that's me sitting in all that garbage. I know, I know . . . I shouldn't be here. But I'm scared. Terrified, actually. Sure, I *want* to go out and perform the poem I wrote about you, but my legs just took off without permission from my brain. They ran away and brought me here to this rubbish heap.

'I need you to help me, Maman. I need some of that heavenly magic. You've got to sprinkle some of it down, 'cause this is an emergency.

'Send me a sign.

'Send help.

'If you think I should go out there, in front of all those people . . . then send someone to find me.'

MISSION IMPOSSIBLE

'We're never going to find him!' said Jaz, throwing up her hands in despair. The clock was ticking and we had all of five minutes to find Aria and convince him to do the performance. But it seemed like an impossible task. He had vanished.

That's when Mum's nose started to twitch. Like in that old TV show *Bewitched*. It always does that when she's working.

'I can smell something,' she said.

'It's the pong from this bin,' replied Jaz, fanning her nose and pointing to the gross blue bin near the stage door. 'That is some funky stench. Let's move.'

Jaz moved away from the bin and towards the theatre. She had given up.

Mum shook her head and kept sniffing. 'No, no, no . . . I can smell something else.' She sniffed her way closer to the bin. 'I can smell . . . saffron!'

Sniff, sniff, sniff . . .

'And rosewater!'

Sniff, sniff, sniff . . .

'I can smell halva!'

Jaz and I looked at each other, stunned. 'You think he's IN the BIN?' I asked.

'There's only one way to find out,' said Mum.

Aria → send me a sign

Just as I had finished talking to Maman, the creaky lid of the bin swung open.

'ARIA!' shouted Hero.

I couldn't believe it. Maman hadn't wasted a single moment. I asked for a sign, and here it was! As ordered, exactly to my specifications. And fast. Maman delivered faster than Amazon!

Hero's mum's supersonic sniffing powers had tracked down the smell of the uneaten, half-squished halva in my pocket. Somehow, she'd recognised that particular smell amid all the other smells of fermented food, used coffee cups and general rubbish that I was sitting in. Her sense of smell really *was* a superpower. Hero had always told me that but I'd thought she was exaggerating . . . until now.

'What the hell are you doing in a dumpster, you big, fat chicken?' said Jaz angrily. She'd never been angry at me before. I didn't understand why she was calling me a big, fat chicken. I'm a boy. Not a chicken. Maybe something was lost in translation?

'Sorry!' I said. 'I panicked, but I'm okay now. Maman sent you guys to find me.'

'It's okay, Aria, it's called stage fright. It happens to lots of people,' said Hero's mum as she extended her hand and helped pull me out of the dumpster.

I apologised again and told them that I was ready now. Ready to face the music, as they say. Jaz smiled – she is quick to forgive.

'You stink. And your shirt is ripped. But that's okay. Let's go kick some butt!'

She grabbed me by the arm and the three of us ran into the theatre, just in time for our performance.

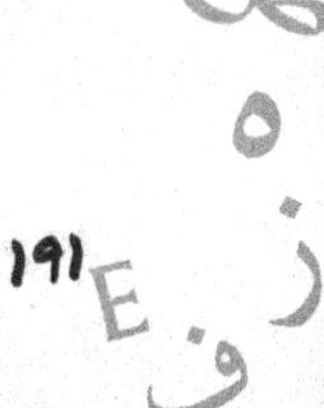

Aria → the abyss

Stepping out onto that stage felt like stepping into an abyss. I didn't know what awaited me. I could hear the announcer calling my name but the sound of his voice echoed in my brain like a dream.

'. . . and making his slam poetry debut, please welcome Aria Hakimiiiiii!'

Jaz, who was wearing her snake Groucho like a coat, gave me a little push onto the stage. 'That's you, my friend. Let's goooo!'

I was nervous but not paralysed anymore. I knew Maman was with me. She was going to help me.

Hero squeezed my arm and smiled. 'You can do this, Aria!'

I put one foot in front of the other, and walked onto the dark stage. Seriously not knowing what awaited me. In that moment, the only force that was operating my movements was faith. I had no logical reason to believe that everything was going to work out. That I would have a voice once I got up to that mic. That I wouldn't freeze, like I always do, and make a complete fool of myself. All I had was faith . . . faith that the stars would somehow align and everything would be okay.

Dreamlike is the only word I can use to explain the feeling as I walked up to the microphone. The stage lights were shining right into my face; I could barely see the crowd. I took a moment to do what Hero's dad had taught me.

A – ACCEPT the madness of this moment.

B – BREATHE . . . I inhaled. I think I sucked up all the oxygen in the theatre.

C – CENTRE my thoughts on Maman.

D – DECIDE. I was here. I was going to do this. This was *my* decision.

E – ENGAGE with the audience. This was my moment.

It seemed like time stood still while I processed all of the above, but I know it happened in just a few seconds.

My eyes adjusted as I looked out into the crowd.

I couldn't believe it. Everyone was there. Not only Baba, Samir and Jaz and Hero's mums, but also half my school. Ms Rubble, our principal Mr Hardball, my ESL teacher Mr Fig, Bruno Barbaro, the fist-bump boy in Year 10, Rufus's commander in-chief Alfie Toogood, and a number of other kids I'd seen around the school, who had never spoken to me but were here now, supporting me, clapping and smiling. I felt my lungs fill up. Not in the way they do when I'm scared or frozen. In a different way. In a way that filled me with hope. As I stood there in front of a room full of people, about to perform, I remembered Maman's words about the power of love. And for the first *real* time since her death, I was feeling it. Feeling it deep, in every fibre of my being.

I took another breath
and stepped up to the mic . . .

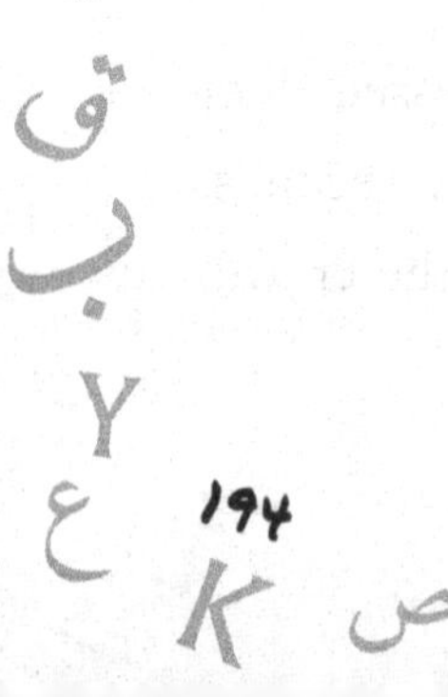

Aria → poetry in motion

Did you know that a microphone can pick up the smallest soundwave, a tiny whisper, and amplify it so that it can be heard a mile away?

I had never heard the sound of my own voice so magnified . . . so clear . . . so loud.

The words came, one after the other. Like they were supposed to. They danced out of my mouth like a conga line of syllables and sounds:

Strong.
Powerful.
Unapologetic.

SLAM DUNK

Aria was ON FIRE!

He had told us during our rehearsal process that he would perform his award-winning poem by himself on the day. That he wouldn't be chiming in with the occasional word like he had been when we busked. That we didn't need to see the poem he'd be performing because he was going to do it solo. It was the only way.

Jaz and I still did our bits, of course. She beatboxed like a pro and I rocked that tambourine but Aria stood front and centre – in front of a crowd of people – and he brought the house down.

This was Aria as we'd never seen him before. He was confident. Loud. Proud. It was as though he was channelling Drake, Amanda Gorman and Eminem all at once. He didn't just read his poem. He slammed it. Slam dunked it. Half recited, half sang, half rapped. Yes, I know that's three halves and hence mathematically not possible, but you get my drift. It was awesome. Jaz and I exchanged amazed looks while accompanying him on stage. Who was he even?

Aria's transformation was out of this world. Everyone could see it . . . and feel it. He broke down all the barriers with his poem. It was about his mother. He was pouring his heart out to the audience and they were mesmerised. I watched as people's expressions shifted. They leant closer. Alert. Present. Some wiped away tears.

It's not that Aria's poem was perfect. It didn't even rhyme. But we all felt it, like an arrow piercing the heart.

I guess you're all dying to hear it?

Okay, here it is. Imagine it kinda rapped, roared, and recited like a boss.

Aria → I am love

Silence you, oh they tried

But they didn't know you

No

Even in death, Maman . . .
 you cannot be silenced

Cover your hair, they said

Lower your voice

Don't look people in the eye

Keep your opinions to yourself

Opinions! You have too many.

It's dangerous, you know.

Know your place, woman

Don't play with fire

Give me the matches, she said

If fighting for my rights, the rights
of my sisters

Is playing with fire, then give me
the matches

Give me the whole damn box

Let's burn this house down

Down to the ground

Until there's nothing left but ashes
and dust

I am not afraid, she said

I am a warrior. I am strong. I am woman.

You will never take away my joy

My hope

My love

For **I am love.**

And love demands justice.

Justice will come.

It will come for you in your sleep.

It is *you* who should be afraid

Sleep with one eye open, my friend

Because tyranny and injustice will never win in the end

It's just not the way of the world

So, you can take my life

But you can never take my voice

For my voice lives on

In the hearts of those I left behind

In my child . . . and my child's child

The voice of justice cannot be silenced

It will rise

And rise again

Until the dawn of a new day

Until the light of peace shines so bright

Until the scars of injustice fade away

And an all-encompassing love swallows
'hate' whole . . . and burps out a
rainbow.

STANDING OVATION

When Aria finished, the crowd sat silently for what seemed like an eternity. His words were still circling the room like magic fairy dust, before gently sprinkling down and landing on each person. A shared understanding spread through the theatre . . . but still no claps.

I got a sinking feeling in the pit of my belly. Was anyone going to clap?

And then, it happened. It started slowly at first, then it got louder and louder. Like a wave of joy covering them all, they erupted into applause. A raucous, roaring applause. It sounded like thunder and rain, like horses galloping and balloons popping. It drowned out all other sounds as it echoed throughout the auditorium and wrapped itself around us like a huge hug.

I felt so proud of Aria, I thought my heart was going to burst. He gestured for me and Jaz to join him front of stage for a bow.

Honestly, in that moment, in that shabby old theatre, it felt like we were the stars of *Hamilton*, the musical.

The applause continued. It swirled around the room, but it wasn't just the sound of hands clapping, it was the sound of love. Aria had moved people with his words. With his performance. He had created a butterfly effect. A mute boy just shared his words with the world (well, our little corner of it, anyway) and it had caused a typhoon.

I wished my dad was here to see all this.

Aria grabbed my hand. Then Jaz's hand.

We took our bow.

This, right here, was the mountain top. If I was feeling this euphoric, I couldn't imagine how Aria must've felt . . .

Aria → a wink from above

I thought my heart was going to explode. I didn't think it was possible to feel this much joy after losing Maman. I looked out into the crowd. Baba was wiping away tears. Samir was standing on his chair, clapping and wolf-whistling. The applause seemed to go on forever. Maman winked at me from above. It's the proudest she's ever been of me.

SCARS

After the pile-on hugs, high fives and celebratory Daggy Dance moves backstage, as we were collecting our things from the communal dressing room and Aria was putting Groucho back into his designer snake cage, I noticed his scarred finger again.

I wondered if he'd ever tell us about it. Tell us about the parts of him that we couldn't see. Those three dents got me thinking about scars in general . . .

Most wounds heal with time. Scars remain. But they're beautiful in their own way. What's Harry Potter without his scar? Or your mama without her stretch marks? And of course, Aria without the mysterious dents on his rude finger?

It's pretty rare to make it through this life with no scars. Not everybody's scars are visible. Some, like Dad's, are perfectly camouflaged.

But they're just as real.

THE AFTERPARTY

Aria wanted to come and see Dad. To thank him. He'd been such a big part of this epic journey and it didn't feel right that he couldn't be there on comp day. I explained that Dad has UPS and DOWNS. That it was okay. He'd missed heaps of my big events too. Ballet concerts, soccer finals, parent–teacher nights. But Aria wasn't disappointed for himself. He was disappointed for Dad and he wanted to do something extra special to thank him.

I knew just the thing! The next morning, Jaz, Aria and I met at Macca's at eight o'clock. Aria could thank Dad by getting him his favourite Macca's meal . . . a stack of extra-hot hotcakes.

Aria decided one serve wasn't enough. He bought six. With his prize money. Oh, I forgot to tell you. He didn't win first prize, which was probably a good thing. Going to Edinburgh would've been a whole to-do.

He won second prize.

$500!

FIVE HUNDRED big ones.

He gave most of it to his dad, but he kept some for us three. We splurged on all kinds of awesome and utterly useless things. Double-dip sherbet candy, Clash Royale coins and pizza.

We asked Awks Macca's Boy to make the hotcakes extra, EXTRA hot because we didn't want them to be cold by the time we got home. Jaz snatched the stack off Aria. She said she couldn't help it. Overnight, she had developed a very rare but real disease called 'Alien Hand Syndrome', where one's hand reaches, grabs and holds on to things without the brain's consent. I shook my head. Classic Jaz.

'Don't you shake your head at me, Hero Jean Rodriguez! It's a REAL condition. Look it up!'

Without meaning to, I rolled my eyes so far back that they did a full loop in their sockets. Maybe I had Alien *Eyeball* Syndrome?

I told Jaz that I believed her but I know that she snatched the stack of pancakes because she wanted to inhale that syrupy goodness through the Styrofoam as we walked back to my house.

Dad was on the couch when we got home. Mum and I joke that he and the couch become besties when Dad isn't feeling the best.

Despite his low mood, Dad's face lit up when he saw us walk through the door.

'Are those hotcakes for me?' he asked.

Jaz plonked them on his lap. 'Extra hot, just how you like them, Mr R.'

Dad smiled and invited us to join him. He couldn't eat six serves. He'd need help. We were happy to oblige. Dad managed to peel his bum off the couch and we sat around the dining room table, Mum and Skye included. We ate hotcakes and filled Dad in on all the amazing slam poetry moments from the previous day.

Jaz cacked herself as she told Dad about Alfie Toogood's comment as we were leaving. She put on her best thug voice and imitated Alfie: 'Way to turn your negatives into positives, bruh. That's full inspirational, bruh. You're the full package, lad!'

Dad actually laughed. This was the happiest I've ever seen him in a DOWN cycle. He congratulated Aria maybe a hundred times then suggested we go for a walk in the sun. I was so happy. Sunshine always helps Dad but sometimes it can be hard to convince him to step into the light. And here he was, suggesting it himself.

We polished off our pancakes and headed out. Mum and Skye stayed behind. Skye had decided to create a slip'n'slide for her dolls using the leftover pancake syrup and an old cereal box, so Mum now had to wash it all out before ant farms started forming.

Aria → friends

As we walked along Hero's sunny tree-lined street, I realised how lucky I was. I had not one but *two* best friends. And they had saved me. Jaz and Hero had waltzed into my life, in their goofy, in-your-face kind of way, and made everything better.

I knew that the three of us would stay friends forever. I also knew that I had to tell them about my past. No, my history doesn't define me, but it's a part of who I am. And they deserved to know all of me. I felt ready to talk.

Today was the day.

Today I would tell them everything.

I stopped walking for a moment and looked up, stared directly at the sun, and with squinty eyes, I made a pledge. From that moment on, I would wrestle, sword-fight and karate-chop any kind of hate that tried to creep its way into my heart. I wouldn't let it clog up my arteries ever again. Maman was right. Hate will ruin you.

I had never wanted to admit it, even to myself, but for so long, I had held on to hate . . . the hate I felt for the people, the regime that took Maman away from me. It had burned a hole inside of me.

I'd been robbed of my voice. But now I had it back, and I was never going to let it go again.

Jaz jolted me out of my thoughts with a friendly shove. 'Dude, enough with the sun-gazing. You're gonna burn a hole in your retina.'

'Is that even possible?' asked Hero.

'I'm glad you asked. Yes. Yes, it is. It's called photokeratitis. An actual disease of the eye caused by ultraviolet light.'

Hero slapped her forehead. 'I should never have asked!'

'I'm pretty sure I had it once . . . had to wear an eyepatch to school, do you remember that, Hero?'

'How could I forget your Long John Silver phase?' replied Hero.

As Jaz continued to tell us about the damaging effects of photokeratitis, I thought about how happy I was. I never imagined it would be possible to feel this

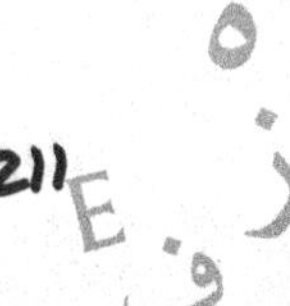

way again. Here I was, in a new land, with new friends and a new life . . . full of possibilities.

I looked up once more. Momentarily. Just long enough to see Maman smiling at me through the piercing rays of the sun.

HERO

I used to think my name was a curse. It seemed cruel that my parents had called me Hero. What a tall order to live up to. Like calling someone 'Impossibly Gorgeous' or 'Astonishingly Brave' or just 'Supergirl'.

But here's what I know now . . .

You don't have to rescue someone from a burning building to be a hero.

You just have to be a friend.

If I died today, my tombstone would say,

Here lies Hero Jean Rodriguez. She was a good friend. And she kicked some serious butt at the tambourine.

And that's good enough for me.

Anahita Rosalind Ghorban-Galaszczuk (yes, that really is her name but you can call her Ana) is discovering that life is absurd. As if dying of cancer at the age of 12.5 isn't bad enough, she still has to endure daily insults from her nemesis, Alyssa (Queen Mean) Anderson.

Ana's on a wild roller-coaster of life and death, kindness and cruelty, ordinary and extraordinary.

And she's got a few things to do before she exits . . .

'Maryam is a brilliantly funny writer for kids. I have asked her to adapt my own books for the stage and she did a magnificent job every time. This original story of hers is an absolute joy.'
- DAVID WALLIAMS